Monster
Mosquitoes
of
Maine

"I'm your biggest fan in the world! I just started your DOUBLE THRILLERS and it's great!"

-Curtis J., Age 11, California

"I just read the book: CURSE OF THE CONNECTICUT COYOTES and it really freaked me out when Erica thought she got attacked by a coyote!"

-Shaina B., Age 10, Minnesota

"I love your books so much that I read everyone in my school library and public library! I hope I get a chance to come to CHILLERMANIA, and I'm saving my money to make it happen. You rock! Keep writing, and I'm your biggest fan!"

-Makayla B., Age 9, Missouri

"Your books are the best I've ever read in my life! I've read over 20 and double thumbs up to all of them!"

-Justus K., Age 11, California

"I never like to read until I discovered your books. The first one I read was VIRTUAL VAMPIRES OF VERMONT, and it totally freaked me out! Me and my friends have our own American Chillers book club. Will you come to one of our meetings?"

-Carson C., age 12, Oklahoma

"I love the American Chillers series I only have three more books to go! My favorite book is HAUNTING IN NEW HAMPSHIRE. It's awesome!"

-Eriana S., age 10, Ohio

"I've read most of your American Chillers books! My favorite was WISCONSIN WEREWOLVES. Right now I am reading KENTUCKY KOMODO DRAGONS. I love it because it is mystery/adventure/chillers! Thank you for writing such exciting books!"

-Maya R., age 9, Georgia

"When we visited my grandparents in San Diego, I found your books at *The Yellow Book Road* bookstore. I bought one and read it in three days! My grandparents took me back to the bookstore and bought me five more! I can't stop reading them!"

-Amber Y, age 11, Hawaii

"I've read every single one of your Michigan and American Chillers and they're all great! I just finished VICIOUS VACUUMS OF VIRGINIA and I think it's the best one yet! Go Johnathan Rand!"

-Avery R., age 10, Delaware

"Your books are the best ones I've ever read! I tried to write my own, but it's hard! How do you come up with so many great books? Please tell me so I can be a writer, too!"

-Lauren H., age 12, Montana

"My family and I were vacationing in northern Michigan and stopped at CHILLERMANIA and you were there! It was the best day of my life!"

-Andrew T., age 8, Tennessee

Got something cool to say about Johnathan Rand's books? Let us know, and we might publish it right here! Send your short blurb to:

Chiller Blurbs
281 Cool Blurbs Ave.
Topinabee, MI 49791

Other books by Johnathan Rand:

Michigan Chillers:

#1: Mayhem on Mackinac Island
#2: Terror Stalks Traverse City
#3: Poltergeists of Petoskey
#4: Aliens Attack Alpena
#5: Gargoyles of Gaylord
#6: Strange Spirits of St. Ignace
#7: Kreepy Klowns of Kalamazoo
#8: Dinosaurs Destroy Detroit
#9: Sinister Spiders of Saginaw
#10: Mackinaw City Mummies
#11: Great Lakes Ghost Ship
#12: AuSable Alligators
#13: Gruesome Ghouls of Grand Rapids
#14: Bionic Bats of Bay City
#15: Calumet Copper Creatures

American Chillers:

#1: The Michigan Mega-Monsters
#2: Ogres of Ohio
#3: Florida Fog Phantoms
#4: New York Ninjas
#5: Terrible Tractors of Texas
#6: Invisible Iguanas of Illinois
#7: Wisconsin Werewolves
#8: Minnesota Mall Mannequins
#9: Iron Insects Invade Indiana
#10: Missouri Madhouse
#11: Poisonous Pythons Paralyze Pennsylvania
#12: Dangerous Dolls of Delaware
#13: Virtual Vampires of Vermont
#14: Creepy Condors of California
#15: Nebraska Nightcrawlers
#16: Alien Androids Assault Arizona
#17: South Carolina Sea Creatures
#18: Washington Wax Museum
#19: North Dakota Night Dragons
#20: Mutant Mammoths of Montana
#21: Terrifying Toys of Tennessee
#22: Nuclear Jellyfish of New Jersey
#23: Wicked Velociraptors of West Virginia
#24: Haunting in New Hampshire
#25: Mississippi Megalodon
#26: Oklahoma Outbreak
#27: Kentucky Komodo Dragons
#28: Curse of the Connecticut Coyotes
#29: Oregon Oceanauts
#30: Vicious Vacuums of Virginia
#31: The Nevada Nightmare Novel
#32: Idaho Ice Beast
#33: Monster Mosquitoes of Maine

Freddie Fernortner, Fearless First Grader:

#1: The Fantastic Flying Bicycle
#2: The Super-Scary Night Thingy
#3: A Haunting We Will Go
#4: Freddie's Dog Walking Service
#5: The Big Box Fort
#6: Mr. Chewy's Big Adventure
#7: The Magical Wading Pool
#8: Chipper's Crazy Carnival
#9: Attack of the Dust Bunnies from Outer Space!
#10: The Pond Monster
#11: Tadpole Trouble

Adventure Club series:

#1: Ghost in the Graveyard
#2: Ghost in the Grand
#3: The Haunted Schoolhouse

For Teens:

PANDEMIA: A novel of the bird flu and the end of the world
(written with Christopher Knight)

American Chillers Double Thrillers:

Vampire Nation & Attack of the Monster Venus Melon

AMERICAN CHILLERS

AMERICA'S #1 SERIES FOR MAXIMUM CHILLS!

#33: Monster Mosquitoes of Maine

Johnathan Rand

An AudioCraft Publishing, Inc. book

Book storage and warehouses provided by Chillermania!© Indian River, Michigan

American Chillers #33: Monster Mosquitoes of Maine
ISBN 13-digit: 978-1-893699-57-1

Librarians/Media Specialists:
PCIP/MARC records available **free of charge** at
www.americanchillers.com

Cover illustration by Dwayne Harris
Cover layout and design by Sue Harring

Printed in USA

Monster
Mosquitoes
of
Maine

VISIT
CHILLERMANIA!

WORLD HEADQUARTERS FOR BOOKS BY JOHNATHAN RAND!

Visit the HOME for books by Johnathan Rand! Featuring books, hats, shirts, bookmarks and other cool stuff not available anywhere else in the world! Plus, watch the American Chillers website for news of special events and signings at *CHILLERMANIA!* with author Johnathan Rand! Located in northern lower Michigan, on I-75! Take exit 313 . . . then south 1 mile! For more info, call (231) 238-0338. And be afraid! Be veeeery afraaaaaaiiiid . . . .

I might as well admit it now: much of what happened to me and my friend, Abby McClure, was all my fault. Our friends dared us to go to the haunted house at the end of Mulberry Street, stand on the porch, and take a picture for proof. We weren't scared, because Abby and I don't believe in ghosts. We didn't believe anything we heard about all the strange things that people said happened there over the years. Actually, I don't think there's any such thing as a haunted house, which is why I decided to take the dare. So did Abby.

But this story, of course, isn't about a haunted house. It's about insects—ordinary mosquitoes—and the horrifying thing that happened to us.

And I know what you're wondering, and you're probably snickering as you read this. You're probably wondering what could be so horrifying about itty-bitty mosquitoes.

Well, I'll tell you.

Nothing.

There's nothing horrifying about itty-bitty mosquitoes.

It's the *monster* mosquitoes I'm talking about. Just how big are they? Spread your arms as wide as you can. More.

Even *more.*

That's how big they are. Monster mosquitoes bigger than eagles and vultures. Some of them have razor-sharp stingers that are over two feet long.

Those are the mosquitoes I'm talking about. When their wings flap and they're buzzing in the air, they sound like airplanes. Their bellies are big enough to hold gallons and gallons of blood that they've sucked from their helpless victims.

These are mosquitoes you can't simply swat. You can't swish them away with a quick sweep of your arm. They don't go away if you happen to hit one with the back of your hand. Matter of fact, if one of these monster mosquitoes gets close enough for you to swat it, it's already too late. Not for them . . . for *you*.

But if Abby and I hadn't accepted that silly dare, if we hadn't gone to the supposed 'haunted' house at the end of Mulberry Street, you wouldn't be reading this story. And Abby wouldn't be plagued by the nightmares she has just about every night.

And I would probably be a normal kid who goes outside, goes camping and hiking in the woods like other kids my age, without the slightest worry about something so pesky as a tiny mosquito.

But I know better.

My name is Ray Carter. This is my story. This is how Abby and I discovered the Monster Mosquitoes of Maine and how we had to fight the toughest battle we'd ever faced . . . just to stay alive.

2

"You're a chicken, Ray, and that's all there is to it."

I rolled my eyes. "Hardly," I said. "There's just no such thing as ghosts, and that old house at the end of Mulberry Street isn't haunted. Everyone just *says* that."

There were four of us that afternoon: me, my best friend Abby, Doug Palmer, and Eddie Grimes.

We were seated on our bikes in the shade of

a huge tree in the park, which isn't far from where we all live in the town of Augusta, which is a city about forty miles northeast of Portland. Augusta is also the state capital.

We'd been talking about the house at the end of Mulberry Street, which is about a mile away. For years, stories have been told about the old house being haunted. It's been for sale for as long as I can remember. Most of the paint has chipped away, the grass in the front yard is overgrown, and I have to admit: it really *does* look creepy.

But that doesn't mean it's haunted, and it doesn't prove there are any ghosts there. As I've already said: I don't believe in ghosts, and neither does Abby.

And that's why Doug and Eddie dared us to go to the house and stand on the porch.

"Let's do it, Ray," Abby said. "Let's go stand on the porch. Nothing's going to happen."

"Fine with me," I said. "I'm not afraid of that old place."

"We'll follow you and watch," Eddie said.

"Why don't *you* guys join us on the porch?" Abby asked.

Doug and Eddie shook their heads.

"No way," Doug said. "That place gives me the creeps."

"Me, too," Eddie agreed. "Why, I heard . . . ."

And he spent the next five minutes telling us all about the horrible things that had happened there, about all of the ghosts that haunt the house. Abby and I listened, and every once in a while, we would glance at each other and roll our eyes.

After Eddie finished, we began pedaling down the street, heading for Mulberry Street. Abby and I were certain that we would prove Doug and Eddie wrong. We were certain there was nothing at that old house that could possibly freak us out.

Man, were we in for a surprise.

3

It took us less than ten minutes to reach the house. We turned into the driveway and rolled to a stop. Doug and Eddie stayed behind us; they didn't want to get too close to the house.

If someone had pulled up right behind us at that moment, they would have seen a curious sight: two rows of four bikes with me and Abby in the front, Doug and Eddie behind us, all peering up at the aging, two-story home with the unmown lawn and the blue and white 'For Sale' sign planted in the front yard. The grass was so tall that the sign was barely visible.

Without a word, Abby and I slid off our bikes and gently laid them down on the cracked cement driveway.

Abby turned and looked at Doug and Eddie.

"Wanna join us?" she asked again with a dry smile.

"Are you kidding?" Doug replied as he shook his head from side to side. "That place is haunted. I'm not getting near it."

"I wouldn't touch it with a ten-foot pole," Eddie said.

"Hey," I said, "you were the one calling me and Abby 'chickens.'"

"We've already been on the porch," Eddie said. "Last summer. That's when we saw the ghost in the window."

"He came after us," Doug said with a nod.

I rolled my eyes. "It was probably the reflection of a bird," I said.

"Believe what you want," Doug said. "The place is haunted. And I bet you can't stay sixty seconds on the porch before you both run away, screaming your heads off."

"Or maybe the ghost will get you," Eddie said.

"Come on, Abby," I said with a grin.

Abby smiled, and together we walked up the driveway to the house, turning onto the narrow cement walkway that led to the porch. Here, the weeds and grass had grown so tall that they bent over the path like thin, green tongues, and the vegetation licked at our jeans.

"This place really needs a good mowing," I said. "Nobody's going to buy a place that looks this ugly."

"Maybe that's why it's been for sale for so long," Abby said.

I turned to see Doug and Eddie watching us from their bicycles in the driveway.

Goofballs, I thought. *They actually believe in ghosts.*

We reached the porch and stopped. I had to admit, the house *did* look a little spooky, with its paint-chipped siding and dirty, smudged windows. I stared into the living room window and imagined the image of a ghost staring back at me, waiting for me to get closer . . . .

"Well?" Doug shouted. "Are you going to step onto the porch or just stand there staring?"

"Maybe you're scared," Eddie sang.

I frowned and stepped up onto the porch. Abby followed. Then, we turned to face Doug and Eddie.

"Start counting out loud," I said loudly.

"One," Doug began, "two, three . . . ."

"This is so silly," Abby said. "They actually think this place is haunted. Too funny."

Then, Doug suddenly stopped counting. He was supposed to count to sixty, but he stopped at twenty-two. His jaw fell, and Eddie's expression was identical.

Without a word, Doug and Eddie spun on their bikes and began pedaling faster than I have ever seen them pedal in their lives. Soon, they'd crested the hill and were gone.

"What was that all about?" Abby asked.

I shrugged. "I have no idea," I said.

Then, we heard a slight squeak behind us. Abby and I turned and could only watch in horror as the old, decaying front door began opening all by itself!

Abby and I just stood on the porch, our bodies immobilized by fear. While we watched, the front door slowly opened. Ancient hinges groaned and squeaked, and it sounded like the door was going to fall over . . . or fall apart right before our very eyes.

I was barely aware that Abby had grabbed my arm until her nails were pinching my skin. Even then, I couldn't do anything about it. I was so terrified by the opening door that I couldn't move.

Then, a ghostly figure appeared. The dark silhouette of a man.

I had seen enough. I wasn't hanging around anymore, and I was just about to turn and run from the house when a voice spoke my name.

"Ray? Ray Carter? Is that you?"

I paused, looking at the man who emerged through the doorway. He looked a little familiar, but I couldn't be sure.

And he most definitely *wasn't* a ghost.

"Aren't you Ray Carter, Tony Carter's boy?"

"Yeah," I said, still a bit confused.

Abby was still squeezing my arm, and I shook it so she would release her grip. Her nails left red welts on my skin.

"I'm Mr. Henderson," the man said. "I'm the realtor who's selling your house."

Suddenly, I remembered him. My parents had put our house up for sale, and Mr. Henderson was the realtor who was helping. Mom and Dad said we were going to move to a bigger home after it sold.

"Oh, yeah," I replied. "Wow! You sure scared us!"

"Sorry about that," he said as he closed the door behind him. "I have several listings on this street, and this is one of them. I come by once in a while to check on the vacant houses."

Abby spoke. "But where's your car?" she asked.

Mr. Henderson pointed down the street. "A few blocks away, parked at the Anderson house. I just left it there and walked here. By the way," he continued, glancing at each of us, "what are *you* two doing here?"

"It was a dare," I replied truthfully. "Our friends say the place is haunted, and they dared us to stay on the porch for sixty seconds."

"Hahahaha!" Mr. Henderson laughed, throwing his head back. "You know, that old rumor about this house has been going on since I was a kid like you two. No truth to it at all. Fun to make up stories, though."

"We don't believe in ghosts," Abby said.

Mr. Henderson looked at Abby.

"Well, now," he said, frowning, "not so fast, not so fast. Don't be too sure of yourself. I used to think the same thing. But then, some friends and I found the old abandoned Hooper farm a few miles from here. Saw some things there that curled our hair."

"Like what?" I asked.

"Oh, scary stuff," Mr. Henderson replied. "Ghosts, I guess. Not sure. But we saw things move on their own and heard strange noises, even during the day. We even went inside, once. Me and my friends, we got so scared, we never went back. Ever."

I looked at Abby, and she looked at me. I knew she was thinking the same thing I was.

"Just where is this place?" she said, stealing the question from my lips.

"Oh, about three, maybe four miles up the old power line trail. When you get to a big pond, you gotta turn right and head another mile. Can't miss the farm."

After a few minutes of chatting, Mr. Henderson left.

Seated on our bikes, Abby and I watched him walk along the side of the road until he disappeared over the hill.

"I still don't believe in ghosts or haunted houses," Abby said.

"Me, neither," I replied. "But I think it would be fun to check out that old farmhouse."

"Do you think he was just making it up?" Abby asked. "My uncle likes to make things up like that, just to fool kids."

"I know how we can find out," I said. "Let's go check it out ourselves."

That little decision was about to get us into big, big trouble. Trouble . . . with a capital 'M.'

5

It was another few days before we could set out to find the supposed 'haunted' farmhouse, because of the weather. It rained for three days straight. Not a heavy rain, but hard enough to keep us from going outside and venturing through the woods.

Finally, on Saturday, I awoke to beautiful sunshine and a crystal blue sky. And it was supposed to be a hot day, too.

Mom made me a couple of sandwiches, and

I tossed them into my backpack, along with a couple of candy bars and two bottles of water.

I met up with Abby in front of the old house at the end of Mulberry Street. She had her own backpack with a lunch and snacks.

"I've been thinking about this," Abby said as we rode down the road, looking for the power line trail. "Even if we don't see any ghosts, we can still make up a story and fool Doug and Eddie. I bet they would believe us."

I laughed. "Maybe we could dare them like they dared us," I replied. "But they probably think that the house at the end of Mulberry Street is really haunted. They took off on their bikes before they saw Mr. Henderson. They probably still think he was a ghost."

Abby laughed. "That was funny!" she said.

It took a bit of searching, but we finally found the trail. It was overgrown with weeds and shrubs, and it appeared no one had used it in a long time. We followed it for a while, and the thick vegetation ate at our legs and bicycle wheels. A couple of times, thick reeds got caught in our bike chains, and we had to stop and pull them out.

"How far do you think we've gone?" Abby asked. We'd been on the trail for nearly thirty minutes.

"Not quite two miles," I said. "But we should be close. Keep your eyes open for that pond Mr. Henderson told us about."

We found it easily enough. Although there were quite a few trees growing up around it and most of the body of water was nearly hidden from view, we could make out the sunlight glinting on its smooth surface.

"This is where we turn to the right and go for about a mile," I said.

"There must be an easier way," Abby said as she wiped a sheen of sweat from her forehead with the back of her arm. We stopped to rest on the trail before starting out in the other direction, where the trail was even fainter and more overgrown.

"I'm sure there is," I answered. "The problem is, we'd probably have to pedal all the way around to the other side and come in from the other direction. That would take us just as long, or longer."

We both sipped water from the bottles in our packs, and we were just about ready to start out again.

"Hey, look at that thing!" Abby said, pointing. Her finger was moving in the air in quick fashion, and I couldn't see what she was pointing at.

"What is it?" I asked.

"It's a mosquito," she replied. Then, I could see it. The thing buzzed in the air near her shoulder. It was big, too, nearly the size of a June bug. When it landed on her arm, she smacked at it and missed, and the creature buzzed away.

"That was the biggest mosquito I've ever seen," she said.

And that was the very moment when a dark shadow appeared from above . . . .

6

Abby and I craned our necks back, looking up into the blue sky. Several small, white, puffy clouds appeared, but the rest of the sky was a beautiful, unblemished blue.

"Check that out," I said, pointing.

Just above the treetops, a turkey vulture was soaring, his wide wings spread to their full extent. We see many turkey vultures in Maine, but they are very skittish, and you usually can't get very close to them. Likewise, they don't like to get near humans if they can help it. Which was why I was so surprised to see this bird so close.

He didn't stay for long. Once he saw us, he flapped his wings and rose into the sky, made several circles, and finally disappeared over the tree line.

"That was cool," Abby said. "He was so close that I could see his individual feathers."

"I wonder if there's a dead animal nearby," I said. "Last week, we were driving to my uncle's house, and we saw four big turkey vultures picking at a dead deer on the side of the highway."

"Oh, gross," Abby said. "Let's talk about something else."

We started out again, following the faint trail as it wound through a field and over a hill. On the other side of the hill, trees began to grow. At first, there were only a few here and there. Gradually, they grew closer and closer together, tighter and tighter, until we found ourselves in a thick forest.

And the farther we traveled, the harder it was to see the trail. It was obvious no one had used it for a long time, and I wondered who had made it in the first place, all those years ago. Perhaps hunters, or perhaps it was an old deer trail.

Finally, we reached a point where it was nearly impossible to see the trail or which way it went. Abby and I stopped.

"It looks like it goes off that way," Abby said.

I shook my head. "But look over there," I said. "You can see where the ground is beat down a little bit. I think it goes that way."

"Either way," Abby said, "we have to be careful. I don't want to get lost."

"We're not going to get lost," I said. "The forest isn't that big. If we get lost, all we have to do is keep going in one direction. Sooner or later, we'll come to a house or a highway. We'll be able to figure out how to get home from there."

"Yeah, but still," Abby said. "I've been lost in the woods before, and I don't like it. I don't want to do it again."

"Don't worry," I assured her. "The last thing we're going to do is get lost. There's nothing to get freaked out about."

We followed the trail in the direction in which I had pointed, and not long after that, we came to a hill. In the distance, there were two things that we noticed that captured our attention.

The first thing we saw, seated on a flat portion of land about a quarter of a mile distant, was the farmhouse that Mr. Henderson had told us about. We couldn't see it all that well, but we were close enough to make out the sagging roof, the boarded-up windows, and the tall weeds and shrubs growing around it. It was shaded by enormous trees that spiraled up into the blue sky. Even from where we were, the place looked creepy—much creepier than the supposed haunted house on Mulberry Street.

Between us and the house, however, was something else:

A marshy pond. It was filled with reeds and

cattails and other water vegetation. I could only imagine the number of turtles, frogs, and toads filling the swamp, just waiting for me to catch them.

But at that very same swamp, something else was there, waiting to catch us.

7

"Mr. Henderson was right," Abby said. "There really is an old farmhouse out here."

"Yeah," I agreed, "but do you think it's haunted? Do you really think he was serious?"

Abby shook her head. "He seemed like a nice guy and all that," she said, "but all that stuff about ghosts and things that go bump in the night is just make-believe. I mean, come on. Lots of people say they *see* ghosts, but no one ever gets a clear picture of any of them. You'd think we'd have figured out a better way to get pictures of ghosts, if there are so many haunted houses in the world and so many ghost hunters."

Abby had a point. I'd watched several ghost hunting shows on television, and I always wondered why the people always search for ghosts at night. Don't ghosts ever come out during the day?

The going was tough on our bicycles, because the grass and shrubbery grew thick and tight. If there was any sign of the trail, we didn't see it, and it sure didn't look like we were following any sort of path. The only thing we could do was push our bicycles around saplings and stumps.

We approached the marshy swamp. It was choked with a lot of vegetation.

"Hold on a second," I said, stopping my bike.

"What's up?" Abby asked.

"I want to see if I can find any frogs or turtles," I said.

"I thought we were looking for ghosts," Abby said.

"We are," I said. "But it's not even noon. We have all day. There might be some big turtles in this pond."

"And what are you going to do if you catch one?" Abby asked. "Take him home? Keep him as a pet?"

"No," I said. "It would just be cool to catch one and see what he looks like."

"You see one turtle, you've seen them all, that's what I say," Abby said.

I hopped off my bicycle and waded through the thick marsh grass. The ground beneath my feet was wet and spongy, and I moved slowly, wary of soft muck. The last thing I wanted to do was step into black goop and get my tennis shoes wet and dirty.

I stopped. My eyes scanned the surface of the pond. Cattails and reeds sprang from the surface like limbless trees.

But I didn't see any turtles, nor did I see any

frogs. In fact, I didn't see any life at all, except for two mosquitoes that seemed unusually large.

Of course, I thought nothing of it. Everyone has seen mosquitoes. Plus, Abby had shooed away a big mosquito earlier in the day.

"See anything?" Abby asked.

"Nothing," I said, shaking my head. "Just a couple of mosquitoes."

I was just about to turn and walk back to my bicycle when a sound caught my attention.

A buzzing sound.

It wasn't like a bug or a bee, but it had the same vibrations. It almost sounded like a lawnmower or a leaf blower.

Abby heard it, too.

"What's that?" she asked.

"I don't know," I replied. "I can't see anything. But whatever it is, it's nearby, in the swamp."

Then, on the other side of the pond, I saw some cattails move. Some reeds fluttered and were knocked down.

Then, something began to rise into the air.

"Oh, my gosh," Abby breathed. *"Oh, my gosh."*

As for me, I couldn't speak. I refused to believe what I was seeing.

8

On the other side of the swamp, something was rising into the air. At first, I thought it was a bird, perhaps a vulture like we'd seen earlier, or maybe a hawk or an eagle.

However, birds like that usually take off in a burst and fly horizontally in a flurry of flapping wings. This creature was moving straight up, slowly and methodically, like a helicopter or a balloon.

And as it cleared the brush, there was no mistaking what it was.

"Is that . . . is that what I *think* it is?" Abby stammered.

"No," I said, shaking my head. "It can't be. There is no way that thing is a mosquito."

But as the insect rose into the air, all other possibilities were quickly eliminated. Sure, I'm only twelve years old, but I've seen enough mosquitoes to know a mosquito when I see a mosquito.

And what we were looking at was most definitely a mosquito. The biggest, nastiest, meanest-looking mosquito I have ever seen in my life.

"I can't believe I'm seeing this," Abby said. "Tell me I'm not seeing this."

"Okay," I said. "You're not seeing this."

"That didn't help," she replied. "It's still there."

We watched while the enormous mosquito continued rising into the air, every once in a while wavering back and forth. Its wings were a blur as it rose higher and higher. Its long legs dangled beneath its fat body, and its stinger was long, narrow, and needle-like. Its stinger was easily two feet long, or longer.

"That thing is as big as a garbage can," I said. "I never knew mosquitoes could get that big."

"They can't," Abby said. "They just can't."

I had a sudden recollection of a book I read the previous year. It was about a boy who shrank and became very small. Normal, everyday creatures became threats. Because he was so small, he had to battle ants, grasshoppers, caterpillars, and even a mouse. He shrank, and everything else around him was enormous compared to his tiny size.

Abby and I certainly hadn't shrunk, but I had the same feeling. The mosquito that was rising into the sky was huge, and I felt very, very small.

"Let's get out of here," Abby said. "We have to tell someone about this. A mosquito that big could kill someone."

Abby had a point. If that mosquito came

after someone, it wouldn't be easily brushed away. A mosquito that big could suck gallons of blood from a human's body. No one could lose that much blood and survive. No one.

The mosquito stopped and hovered about fifty feet off the ground. It was facing the other way, so I didn't think it'd spotted us.

"Let's wait just a minute," I said. "Maybe he'll go away."

We stood in the sunshine, watching the monster mosquito as it hovered over the swamp.

"It's almost like he's watching something," Abby said. "It's like he's looking at something on the ground."

My eyes scanned the swamp, and I saw something move near the edge on the other side.

A rabbit.

I could see his head poking through the reeds. He was crouched at the edge of the swamp with his nose near the surface of the water. He was getting a drink.

In a horrifying moment of realization, I

knew what the mosquito was doing. He was waiting for the right moment to strike

"Right there," I said, nodding. "There's a rabbit on the other side of the swamp. He sees the rabbit."

Abby gasped. "That poor rabbit!" she said. "He won't have a chance against that thing! Even if he tries to run, he's not going to outrun a mosquito that big!"

Without warning, the mosquito dropped out of the sky like a diving bird of prey, rocketing down with amazing speed. The insect's long, needle-like stinger was pointed downward, its wings were flared back, and its sights were set on the helpless, furry creature that had no idea of the danger in the sky.

Now, it was *my* turn to gasp. We were about to witness an act of barbaric, ruthless cruelty. Abby was right: that poor bunny rabbit wasn't going to stand a chance.

9

Without even thinking about the consequences, I suddenly began waving my arms in the air.

"Hey!" I shouted.

It worked. My sudden movement and shout scared the rabbit. He turned and quickly vanished in the weeds.

But the mosquito wasn't going to give up. He changed his course and skirted over the brush, zigzagging back and forth, hot on the trail of the retreating rabbit. His wings buzzed like a saw as he chased down the fleeing rodent.

Soon, however, it was apparent that the rabbit had gotten away. Perhaps he'd found his hole in the ground or someplace else to hide in the thick brush. Whatever he had done, it worked, because the giant mosquito slowed his movements. He hovered in different spots, as if he was searching for signs of the rabbit.

"I think the bunny got away," I said.

"That was quick thinking," Abby said. "I thought that mosquito was going to spear him with its stinger."

We watched the mosquito as it continued to canvass the weeds and bushes, searching for the rabbit.

"I can't believe I'm seeing this," Abby said. "I can't believe a mosquito grew that big."

I shook my head. "I can't either," I said. "It must be some sort of mutated insect. It certainly isn't a normal mosquito, that's for sure," I said.

Abby spoke. "Let's get out of here before

it—"

Whatever Abby was going to say, she didn't get a chance to finish. She stopped speaking when the mosquito made a sudden loop and turned toward us. It hovered for a minute, swayed to the left and then to the right, then began flying in our direction.

"Let's get out of here!" I said.

Quickly, we turned our bikes around and were about to flee, but I quickly realized that there was no way we would be able to outrun the mosquito, especially on our bikes. It was simply too fast, and the area around us was too overgrown with weeds and brush.

"He's going to get us!" Abby panicked.

I jumped off my bicycle and crouched down behind it. *"Get off your bike!"* I shouted. *"Hide behind it!"*

Abby did as I told her. "But he can still see us!" she shouted as she hunkered down behind her bike.

"Maybe so," I said, "but we can use our bikes

as shields. We have nothing else to use to defend ourselves."

It was a good thing we acted as quickly as we did, as the monster mosquito was even faster than I thought. Abby had no sooner hidden behind her bicycle than the mosquito was upon us. It dove down at me, and I grabbed my bicycle, wielding it like a shield. The mosquito slowed and swooped back up into the sky, readying for another assault.

This time, the insane insect went after Abby. His long stinger shot down like a javelin. I couldn't believe how fast it was.

That stinger could go right through one of our arms or legs, I thought. *Or right through our stomachs!*

Abby screamed. The only protection she had was her bicycle, and that wasn't very much.

Just as the mosquito was about to reach her, I threw my bicycle, as best I could. It was heavy, and I couldn't throw it very far, but I had to do something to try to block the attacking insect.

It was a direct hit. The mosquito was

knocked out of the air, and it tumbled into the grass only a few feet away. I should have run over to it and tried to stomp on it or run it over with my bicycle. But I couldn't. I was too amazed, maybe even a bit dazed, watching the enormous insect as it got to its six legs and rested in the tall weeds.

Abby scrambled to her feet and stood behind her bicycle as she backed up next to me.

The mosquito's wings began flapping, and it slowly rose into the air. It wavered back and forth, and I wondered if I had injured it.

Whatever I had done, the mosquito didn't seem to be interested in us anymore. It rose higher into the sky and slowly flew over the swamp.

"Let's get out of here," Abby said. "We've got to get home and tell somebody about this. That thing could kill somebody!"

"I'm all for that," I said.

We began pushing our bicycles, but had gone only a few feet when I stopped.

Ahead of us, directly in our path, flying several feet off the ground, were two more gargantuan mosquitoes.

Abby saw the insects and gasped.

I turned and looked at the old farmhouse in the distance.

Can we make it? I wondered. *Can we make it to that old house and get inside before those mosquitoes come after us?*

"Let's get to the old house!" I said to Abby. "It's our only chance! There's no way we can fend those things off with our bicycles." I dropped my bike in the grass, slipped out of my backpack, and placed the backpack on the front wheel of my bike. "We've got to get to a place where those things can't get at us. If we can get into that house, we'll be safe."

Abby began to push her bike.

"Leave it!" I said. "Leave it here! We can run faster that way!"

"But what if they come after us?" Abby shrieked as she let go of her bike. Then, she pulled off her backpack and dropped it on the ground. "We don't have anything to defend ourselves with!"

"That's a chance we've got to take!" I said. "Now! Let's go!"

"We're never going to make it!" Abby screamed.

"Well," I shouted back, "we can't just stay here and get speared by those two things! Let's get out of here!"

I took her by the hand, and we began running through the brush. But when I glanced over my shoulder, I saw that my worst fear had come true.

The two mosquitoes were headed toward us.

And they were moving *fast*.

10

"They're coming!" I shouted. "Run faster!"

"I'm running as fast as I can!" Abby shouted.

The house was still some distance away, probably the length of a football field. I had no idea if we would make it in time, but we had no other option.

Even if we make it, I thought, the doors are probably locked. We'll have to force our way inside, *or find another place to hide.*

I pumped my legs as hard as I could, sprinting through the brush, jumping over bushes, and leaping over tree stumps. Abby ran alongside of me. She has always been a fast runner, very athletic, and her strength and speed sure came in handy now.

We made it about halfway to the house when I began to hear the familiar lawnmower-like buzzing sound. I turned around to see not two, but *three* mosquitoes coming after us. It appeared that the one that had chased us earlier had joined the other two, and they were coming at us like a formation of fighter jets.

"We can make it!" I shouted to Abby. Actually, I wasn't sure if we would make it or not, but just saying those words made me feel better, and I hoped it gave encouragement to Abby.

Ahead of us, the house loomed larger as we got closer. It was old and decrepit, and I was certain no one had lived there for a long time. Most of the windows were boarded up. I was certain that we'd find the doors locked.

I don't want to have to break in, I thought, *but if we have to, we will. I'm not going to stay outside and get all of the blood sucked out of me by those giant flying vampires.*

The high-pitched whining sound grew louder and louder, and I was afraid to turn around and look. I knew that the mosquitoes were gaining on us, that they were much faster than we were. I didn't want to turn around to see how close they were. I wanted to focus on getting to the house, on getting inside, on getting safe.

I wasn't aware of it at the moment, but Abby was slowly starting to fall behind. Yes, she was a fast runner, but I was a little faster. She was now a few steps behind me.

"I can't go much farther!" she shouted.

I turned my head for just a moment, to see where she was. She was still running, but she was a few feet behind me and was tiring quickly.

What was worse: the three mosquitoes were very close. Their eyes were dark and focused, and their deadly stingers were aimed at us, ready to strike, ready to puncture our soft flesh. It was truly a horrifying sight.

I slowed just enough to give Abby time to catch up. Then, I grabbed her hand and ran with her, helping her along.

We were almost at the house.

The mosquitoes had almost reached us.

Abby's hand was suddenly yanked from my grip. She screamed and went down. At first, I thought she had tripped, but that's not what happened.

One of the mosquitoes had hit her, knocking her off balance, sending her tumbling into the tall grass and brush. Instantly, the gigantic insect had pinned her to the ground, raised its head back, and poised its long, needle-like stinger, preparing to strike.

Abby screamed. She tried to wriggle free, but the mosquito was too strong. Its six powerful legs held her to the ground. Although she struggled and fought, she was powerless to do anything.

"Abby!" I shouted.

"Help me, Ray!" Abby screamed desperately.

I didn't know what to do. The other two mosquitoes were in the air, but they hadn't attacked yet.

Without thinking, I leapt at the insect in a last-ditch attempt to save Abby's life.

It was too late. The massive monster mosquito was already plunging its stinger down before I had time to do anything.

11

I slammed into the giant bug, and that's what saved Abby's life. His stinger had been only inches from her chest, but the force of my blow knocked the insect off of her. Now, I had fallen on top of it, and it was buzzing and struggling madly, trying to get out from beneath me.

I wanted to get away, too. I rolled sideways and kicked at the insect, which knocked it over once again.

Abby had already leapt to her feet. I jumped up, and we continued running toward the house.

Behind us, the mosquito was rising into the air, where it was joined by the other two. Without hesitation, the three continued their pursuit.

I focused on the house. The front door was closed, and I was certain that it would be locked. No matter. It was old, and I was sure that if I hit it hard enough, I could knock it open.

Twenty feet. In another ten steps, we would be there.

Abby snapped her head around. "They're almost here!" she screamed.

"We can make it!" I shouted.

Then, we were at the house, bounding across the old, decaying porch. Without slowing down, I forced my body squarely into the weathered front door.

A burst of pain rocked my shoulder and upper body. The door seemed to give a little bit, but it held fast. Still, I wasn't going to give up. I backed away, raised my leg, and gave the door a swift kick. Abby, too, joined me. It took several heavy beatings, but the bolt suddenly tore away from the molding, and the door opened with a thundering shudder.

"Inside!" I shouted. We sprang forward, and I turned and slammed the door shut just as the mosquitoes reached us. One of them hit the door, but I used my weight to hold it closed. We could hear them buzzing madly, wildly, just behind the door and the wall.

I fell to the floor with my back against the door. Abby collapsed next to me. She was crying.

"We're okay," I said, trying to comfort her. "We're safe."

And we were. We were safe for the time being. But we couldn't stay in the house forever. At some point, we would have to leave.

But that would be later. For the time being, we just rested, thankful that we were both alive.

12

The inside of the house was only dimly lit by thin shafts of light that leaked through the boarded-up windows. We were in the entryway of a living room that was nearly empty, except for a couple of old dining room chairs. There was no other furniture, nothing hanging from the walls. Opposite us, on the other side of the room, was a large, stone fireplace. All of the ashes had been cleaned out.

After a few minutes, the buzzing ceased. I slowly rolled to my knees, then stood. I grabbed one of the old dining room chairs and carried it to the door. Abby moved out of my way as I tilted the chair and placed its back beneath the doorknob.

"That should hold," I said. "That should keep them out."

I walked to one of the boarded-up windows and peered between the slats.

"Do you see anything?" Abby asked.

I shook my head. "No," I replied. "I can't see very well. But it looks like they're gone."

"I'm sure they're not far away," Abby said.

"Yeah," I agreed. "You're right about that. Now, we've got to figure out what we're going to do."

"If only we had a phone," Abby said. "Then, we could call for help."

I knew that searching for a phone in the old house was pointless. It had been abandoned for far too long. I was certain we wouldn't find a phone, and I was also certain the house didn't have electricity.

So, we would have to figure out something else to do.

"At least we're safe," I said. "For the time being, we're okay."

"But if we go outside, those things are going to get us," Abby said.

"I wonder where they came from," I said. "They look like ordinary mosquitoes, but they're gigantic. I've never heard of mosquitoes growing that big."

"This is like a scary movie," Abby said.

"At least most scary movies have happy endings," I said. "Come on. Let's explore this place. Maybe we'll find something in the house we can use."

"A giant flyswatter would come in handy right now," Abby said, and I laughed.

"Or a giant can of bug killer," I said.

I helped her to her feet, and we walked across the living room. The old wood floor squeaked beneath our feet. We entered the

73

kitchen, which was just as empty as the living room had been. Several of the cupboard doors were open, exposing dark, empty shelves.

"Nothing in here," I said. "Let's keep going."

We walked through the kitchen and into a hallway. We found three bedrooms, but all were completely empty. The only thing the rooms contained was a fine layer of dust on the floor.

At the end of the hall was a staircase that rose up to the second floor.

"Careful," I said. "The house is really old, and the stairs are old, too. Let me go first."

I slowly and carefully took the steps. The ancient wood groaned beneath my feet, but it felt solid enough.

"It's okay," I said. "I think they'll hold."

Together, we went up the stairs to the second floor, where we found two more bedrooms and a large bathroom. Once again, we found nothing that would be of use.

In one of the bedrooms, the window had been boarded up, but one of the slats of wood had fallen away, exposing a large, gaping hole that let in sunlight. I walked toward it and looked outside.

On the other side of the overgrown lawn was something I hadn't seen before: an old shed. Like the house, it, too, looked like it was falling apart.

I saw something leaning against it that made me want to jump up and down and cheer.

"That's it!" I shouted, and my voice echoed in the bedroom, bouncing off the empty walls, floor, and ceiling. "That's just what we need!"

Abby joined me at the window.

"What?" she asked

I pointed and held my finger against the glass.

"Right there," I said. "A pitchfork! Leaning against that old shed! That's just what we need! We can use that thing to fend off the giant mosquitoes!"

The pitchfork would be perfect. It was about six feet long, with sharp, twelve-inch tines. It would be the perfect tool to keep the mosquitoes from getting at us while we escaped.

"Is there another one?" Abby asked.

Our eyes searched the yard and the area around the shed, but we didn't see anything.

"It looks like there's only one," I said.

The problem was that the pitchfork was outside, on the other side of the yard, leaning against the shed.

And getting to it without being attacked by the monster mosquitoes was going to be a challenge.

13

We hurried down the hall, down the stairs, through the living room, and to the front door. I went to several windows and tried to look outside, but because they were boarded up from the outside, there wasn't anything to see.

"I don't hear the mosquitoes buzzing around," Abby said.

"That doesn't mean they're gone," I said. "They might be hiding in the trees nearby, waiting for us to come out."

"Do you think they're that smart?" Abby asked. "I mean, after all, they're just bugs."

"They might be bugs," I replied, "but they know how to survive. And like most mosquitoes, they can probably smell us. They can smell our blood."

Abby shivered. "I just don't understand where they came from," she said.

"I don't, either," I said. "But we'll let someone else figure that out. Right now, we have to think about how we're going to get home."

I pulled the chair away and pushed it aside. Slowly, I opened the door a tiny bit and peered through the crack.

"Do you see any of them?" Abby asked

I shook my head. "No," I answered. "But I can't see much from here."

I opened the door a little bit farther and spotted the pitchfork on the other side of the yard, leaning against the shed. I tried to estimate how long it would take me to get there, how many steps

I would have to take before I reached it.

Fifteen seconds, I thought. *I can make it to the pitchfork in fifteen seconds, grab it, and it will take me another fifteen seconds to get back to the house.*

"I'm going to go get the pitchfork," I said. "Stand by the door and wait for me. Keep it open just a tiny crack, so you can see where I am. When I get back, open it up so I can run inside. As soon as I'm back here, close the door."

"Are you sure this is a good idea?" Abby asked.

"No," I said. "It's not a good idea at all. But considering the circumstances, we have no other option. We can't stay here forever. No one knows we're here, and we have no way of letting anyone know what's going on. We can't call 911 and tell them that giant mosquitoes are attacking us."

"They would probably die laughing and hang up," Abby said.

She was probably right. Even if we had a phone and tried to call for help, no one would believe us.

I turned and glanced at Abby. She looked scared.

"I'll be fine," I said, trying to reassure her. "After all, they're just insects. They're not very smart. They're just trying to survive, like any other bug."

"Be careful," Abby said.

I turned back toward the door and peered out through the crack once again, making another survey of the yard and the nearby trees. Seeing nothing, I opened the door and stepped out onto the porch.

Outside, it was deceptively peaceful. I could hear birds chirping in the trees and crickets chiming from the bushes. A very gentle breeze hissed through the trees, fluttering the bright green leaves.

But I saw no sign of the giant mosquitoes.

Maybe they're gone, I thought. *Maybe they've moved on to someplace else.*

On the other side of the yard, I spied the pitchfork leaning against the shed. All I needed to do was run across the yard and grab it. Then, if one of the mosquitoes came after me, I would at least have some way to defend myself.

I gave one last glance behind me. Abby had closed the door, leaving it open a tiny crack. I could see part of her nose and an eyeball peering back at me.

Then, I looked at the pitchfork, took a breath, and sprang.

I took long, striding steps as I ran through the tall, unmown grass, and I was halfway to the pitchfork when I heard a scream.

Abby.

Then, I heard the now familiar, high-pitched whine of enormous, fluttering wings.

Instead of turning around to see where the mosquito was, I kept my entire focus on the pitchfork. It was my lifeline. If I didn't have the pitchfork, I would be completely defenseless.

I wasn't going to make it.

A stab of pain shot through my shoulder, and I was sent stumbling forward, off balance and out of control. I fell face-first into the tall grass, but before I could get up, six legs grasped my body and forcefully pinned me to the ground. My face was buried in the earth, and I couldn't see a thing. Abby screamed one more time, and I managed to twist around to see my attacker . . . just as the stinger came down to puncture my neck.

14

Just the thought of that razor-sharp javelin piercing my flesh sent a wave of adrenaline surging through my body. I turned my head and twisted to the right, just in time to prevent instant death. The monster mosquito's stinger missed my neck, but it caught part of my T-shirt. Not only that, but the stinger drilled into the soft earth. When the mosquito tried to pull back, he found that he was stuck. Its stinger was buried nearly ten inches into the ground, pinning me down by my T-shirt.

I had an idea. Being that the insect couldn't harm me as long as its stinger was buried in the ground, I thought I was safe. Yes, it was pretty gross having a giant bug on top of me, pinning me to the ground with his legs, but I didn't have time to worry about that.

Instead, I freed my arms and raised them up, wrapping both hands behind the mosquito's volleyball-sized head. I began pulling the insect toward me in an effort to keep his stinger stuck to the ground. As long as he was stuck, he couldn't hurt me.

This infuriated the mosquito. His wings fluttered like mad, and the sound was deafening. It was like a leaf blower right next to my head.

And he was strong, too. He tried to force himself away with his legs and pull back with his head, but I held fast. Sure, I was pinned to the ground right along with him, but my plan was working. Without the use of his stinger, the mosquito couldn't hurt me.

"Ray!" Abby shouted. *"Watch out! There's another one coming!"*

Above, I saw the dark shadow of another mosquito approaching. He hung in the air like a helicopter, watching carefully, waiting for the perfect moment to attack.

And I knew there was no way I would be able to fend him off. I was too busy with the mosquito that had me pinned to the ground. Because my T-shirt was stuck, I had no way to flee. Even if I could kill the insect, I would still have to remove the stinger from the ground so my shirt would be released.

In the sky, the monster mosquito must've figured that it was the right time to strike, because he suddenly dove down, dropping like a rock, heading straight for me.

Without any way of defending myself, I knew that it was all over. I was helpless. Trying to get the pitchfork had been a good idea, but I had failed . . . and now I was going to pay the price.

15

The mosquito was bearing down on me, and I couldn't believe how fast it moved. At the very last moment, I closed my eyes and prepared for the pain.

It never came.

Instead, I heard a loud *thunk*, and the mosquito stopped buzzing. In the same instant, I was covered in wet, greasy goop. It smelled horrible. It was on my face, covering my eyes, nose, and mouth.

When I opened my eyes, I was shocked to see Abby standing above me. Her hair was wild, and her eyes were on fire. She was gasping, out of breath and carrying a five-foot piece of the porch railing from the house. Nearby, a giant mosquito lay in the tall grass. Its body was split open, and bug goop was splattered all over the creature. It was totally gross.

I was still struggling with the mosquito that was pinning me to the ground, unwilling to let him go for fear of him getting me, when Abby shouted.

"Let him go!" she cried. *"Let him go, and I'll knock him silly!"*

I released my grip on the back of the insect's head just as Abby swung the piece of wood. The mosquito, however, was faster and succeeded in pulling his stinger out of the ground and fluttering into the air. Abby's swing swished through the air without connecting with the insect.

But the good thing was that the mosquito didn't return for an attack. Maybe he'd had enough, because he quickly rose into the air buzzing like a radial arm saw.

Ignoring the fact that I had bug goop all over myself, I leapt to my feet. "Get back to the house!" I shouted to Abby. "I'll get the pitchfork! You get back to the house before he comes back again!"

Wordlessly, Abby ran back to the house carrying part of the porch railing. I darted the short distance to the shed and felt a surge of relief and power as I reached the pitchfork. I pulled it from the ground, turned, and began running across the yard. My eyes scanned the skies, the trees, and around the house for any sign of the monster mosquitoes. I didn't see any except for the dead insect in the grass, and as I bounded across the porch to the front door, relief once again welled up through my body.

Abby opened the front door, and I plunged inside. She closed the door behind me and pressed her back to it, using her weight to keep it shut.

I stopped in the middle of the living room and leaned on the pitchfork, gasping for breath.

"That thing almost got you," Abby said, pointing to my shoulder.

I looked down. There was a huge hole in my T-shirt from where the stinger had gone through.

"That could've been my neck or my chest," I said. "And if it hadn't been for you, that other one would have killed me for sure."

"I couldn't just stand there and watch that happen," Abby said.

"Using that piece of railing was a great idea," I replied.

"I didn't know if it would work or not," she said. "But I had to try."

I raised my right arm, disgusted by the goop on my skin. It was a mix of red, green, and white liquid, and it was so gross looking, so gross smelling, that I thought I was going to throw up.

"I've got to get washed off," I said.

"Sorry about that," Abby said.

"Don't be sorry," I replied. "If it hadn't been for you, I'd be dead right now. I'd rather have bug juice on me than have that creature stab me with his stinger."

I leaned the pitchfork against the wall and walked into the kitchen. There was no running water, of course, but I searched the cupboards and was lucky enough to find an old dish towel someone had left behind. I used it to wipe off my face and arms. As for my T-shirt, there wasn't much I could do about it. But at least I got the gooey stuff off my face and out of my eyes.

I walked back into the living room. Abby was still leaning with her back against the front door.

"Now what?" she asked.

"We make a plan," I said. "Now that I have a pitchfork and you have a piece of wood, we have a way to defend ourselves. You've already killed one mosquito, and we know that there are at least two more."

"Listen," Abby said. "I can hear one of them."

I slowly walked toward her, listening. Somewhere outside, I could hear the now familiar

91

high-pitched whine of at least one monster mosquito buzzing around in the air.

The sound became louder.

Louder still.

Closer.

All too late, I realized what was about to happen.

"Get away from the door!" I shouted frantically. "Get away! Now! *Now!*"

It was too late. With a thundering explosion, the door was blown in as the mosquito smashed into it. Abby was knocked to the ground, and the piece of railing she had been carrying went flying across the room.

The monster mosquitoes had begun their counterattack.

16

In seconds, I had grabbed the pitchfork. Holding it with both hands, I ran across the living room, aiming the sharp tines at the mosquito that had knocked in the door. He was on the floor, standing on all six legs, with his stinger pointed directly at Abby, who was still sprawled out on her stomach. The wind had been knocked out of her, and she was struggling to catch her breath.

Now, it was my turn to help her.

Fearless, I held the pitchfork in front of me and made an all-out assault on the mosquito. If Abby had been able to kill one of them with a piece of deck railing, I was certain I could do the same with a pitchfork.

The mosquito, however, anticipated my attack and suddenly retreated out the front door, buzzing into the air, up, up, and vanishing over the roof.

I dropped the pitchfork, and it clanked to the floor. Then, I lifted up the front door and replaced it as best I could in the doorway. I kept my eye on it as I knelt next to Abby.

"Are you okay?" I asked.

Abby rolled to her side, still gasping and wheezing.

"I . . . I can't . . . can't . . . b . . breathe," she stammered. Her voice was choked, and it was difficult for her to speak.

"Don't try to say anything," I said. "Just try to catch your breath. You'll be all right."

Outside, I heard the telltale sound of not

one, but two monster mosquitoes. It sounded like they were just above the rooftop.

I stood up, picked up the pitchfork, and faced the door, ready for anything. I knew that the mosquitoes weren't going to give up easily, and I wanted to be ready.

"After you catch your breath," I said, "we'll get out of here. I think we'll be able to fend them off on our own if it's just the two of them. And if we can kill them, that would even be better."

Abby's breathing was becoming easier, and she sat up. She was still gasping, taking slow, deep breaths. I felt bad for her, but at least she was okay. The door had protected her from the mosquito's onslaught, and she was going to be fine.

After a few minutes, Abby got to her feet.

"Just for the record," she said, "I'm not having any fun."

Suddenly, I realized something.

"You know," I said, looking around, "we came here because this place is supposed to be haunted."

"It doesn't look haunted to me," Abby said. "I'm more afraid of the mosquitoes than I am of ghosts."

I shifted the front door and peered outside, looking for any sign of the mosquitoes. I could still hear them, but they sounded far off. Soon, the buzzing sound stopped.

"It sounds like they went away," I said.

"Yeah," Abby said. "But you can bet they'll be back. Especially if we leave this place and go out into the open."

"We don't have any choice," I replied. "Are you ready?"

Abby bent over and picked up the long piece of deck railing. "As ready as I'm ever going to be," she replied.

I leaned the pitchfork against the wall. Grabbing the front door with both hands, I moved it aside, nervously searching the yard and the field beyond for any signs of the mosquitoes. I was relieved when I didn't see anything out of the ordinary.

"Let's move," I whispered.

We stepped out onto the porch, stopped, watched, and listened. Seeing and hearing nothing, we stepped off the porch and into the yard, still scanning the area for any sign of the monster mosquitoes.

"What's the plan?" Abby asked.

"We head back the way we came," I replied. "If we have to, we can leave our bikes and pick them up later. It might be hard to ride them through the woods while carrying a pitchfork and a piece of wood. Keep your eyes open and be ready."

Cautiously, we started out across the yard, heading toward the field and the swamp.

We didn't get far.

17

We hadn't taken more than a dozen steps when we began to hear the mosquitoes again. They were far away, and we couldn't see them yet.

Abby and I stopped, our eyes searching the skies.

"Do you think we should go back into the house?" she asked.

I shook my head. "No," I answered. "We can't stay there forever. We've got to get home, we've got to call the police or somebody." I raised the pitchfork, then motioned toward the long piece of wood Abby was carrying. "At least now we have a way to defend ourselves," I said.

We continued walking, and we could still hear the sound of the buzzing mosquitoes somewhere in the distance. But it was impossible to tell from what direction the sounds were coming or if they were getting closer.

And while we walked, my mind spun. I wondered where the mosquitoes came from, what had caused them to grow to such enormous sizes. Were they normal mosquitoes that had somehow mutated, or were they a different species of insect altogether? I didn't have the answers, and at the time, I really didn't care. I just wanted to get home alive. We could figure out what to do from there.

We had no trouble finding our bikes. They were still laying on their sides in the grass with our backpacks on top of them.

"Let's leave them there," I said. "I don't think anyone is going to steal them."

"If anyone comes out here," Abby said, "they're going to get the surprise of their lives. Anyone who sees those mosquitoes will have nightmares for weeks. I know I will."

When Abby stopped speaking, the buzzing sound suddenly became louder. We stopped walking and searched the sky for the insects.

"It sounds like they're all around us," Abby said.

"Yeah," I said, "but I can't see them. It sounds like they're just beyond the tree line."

"I'm ready," Abby said, gesturing with the piece of deck railing that she was carrying. She raised it up like a gun. "Just let them try to get at us."

We continued walking, and the buzzing sound continued to get louder and louder. It was maddening not knowing from which direction they were coming. I wanted to be ready, but I couldn't be ready if I couldn't see them. We already knew that they were incredibly fast, and I didn't want to be ambushed without being prepared.

"There's one!" Abby suddenly said, making a motion with the piece of wood she was carrying. "Over there, up above the trees."

In the distance, a monster mosquito had risen up above the trees. It hovered in the air, seeming to balance itself perfectly, remaining almost motionless.

"Let's keep going," I said. "Keep watching him, but let's keep moving."

We walked and watched. Another mosquito appeared.

Then another.

And another. More.

Still more.

We stopped and watched, horrified. There were dozens of them, rising and falling, swaying to the left and to the right. Their fluttering wings sounded like a hundred motorcycles revving.

It was a swarm . . . and a very bad day was about to get a lot worse.

18

I wondered whether we should continue on or go back to the old house. If we went back to the house, we would be safe, as long as we could keep the mosquitoes out.

However, if we did that, we'd be no closer to getting home or getting help. Sooner or later, we had to get home. Regardless of whether we were safe, we couldn't stay in that old house forever.

So, I decided we would continue. Without

our bikes, it would take us longer, but at least we had the pitchfork and the piece of deck railing.

"Let's run," I said, and we started jogging. "Be careful not to trip."

I hated to think of that enormous swarm coming after us, and I wondered how we would fend off so many enormous mosquitoes. However, at the moment, they didn't show any signs of coming after us. Maybe they didn't see us yet.

We jogged through the field and made it to the edge of the forest, where we found the faint trail.

Behind us, on the other side of the field and above the trees, the swarm of deadly monster mosquitoes looked as menacing as ever. But they didn't look like they were coming any closer, and I began to think that maybe we would make it home after all. Maybe we wouldn't have to use the pitchfork and the deck railing to defend ourselves.

Another good thing: we didn't have to make it home to be safe. I'd already made up my mind to stop at the first house we found. I was sure we would be able to find someone who would let us use the telephone to call the police and then call home.

I can't believe no one else knows about those mosquitoes, I thought. They had to come from somewhere. If they threatened us, they most certainly would have threatened other humans.

Then again, maybe the mosquitoes stayed in the forest. There weren't any other homes besides the old farmhouse that we'd found, and there weren't any other people around.

And if the mosquitoes weren't feeding on humans, what were they eating? Blood, of course. But from what? A deer? Rabbits?

Probably. I remembered the poor rabbit at the edge of the swamp and how he'd almost been a mosquito meal. I shuddered at the thought of those creatures swarming through the forest with their deadly stingers, attacking animals like they had attacked us.

Now that we were in the forest, we could no longer see the mosquitoes gathering above the trees on the other side of the field. There was some relief with that, but, then again, I liked knowing where they were. If we could at least see them in the distance, we would know they hadn't come after us.

My relief didn't last long.

As we jogged through the forest, we heard one of the mosquitoes approaching. It buzzed overhead, above the trees, and we saw its dark silhouette beneath the sun.

"Okay," I said. "Be ready. We don't know how many of those things are going to come after us."

"Wait a second," Abby said. She stopped and pointed. "Look over there! There's a house or something!"

I looked at where she was pointing. She was right. Through the forest, we could see the gray wall of a house. We couldn't see much, but it was most definitely a structure.

Hopefully, that would mean people. A safe place. A telephone.

The mosquito that had buzzed us once came back again, flying lower this time, zipping in and around tree branches.

"Let's hurry," I said. "Let's try to make it to the house and hope that someone is home."

The sound of a thousand lawnmowers became louder as we changed our course, leaving the trail and pushing our way through and around branches and small saplings. We couldn't run, because there was too much brush in our way. Still, we managed.

But the problem was that the buzzing sound was growing steadily in our ears. It was as if the single monster mosquito had been sent out as a scout to look for us. Now, the entire swarm knew where we were . . . and we were about to face our toughest battle yet.

19

I tried to ignore the loud flapping of mosquito wings and focus on pushing our way through the brush and reaching the house. As we drew closer, we could see that the building was actually a barn, but there was a house next to it.

"Do you see any of them, yet?" Abby asked as she looked up and around. Her voice was tense, filled with fear.

I snapped my head around, looking up and

back, peering through the leafy branches, trying to get a glimpse of anything that moved.

"No," I replied. "But they're getting closer, for sure."

We pressed on. The sound of so many flapping mosquito wings drove me crazy. It was so loud in my ears that I could hardly hear my feet crashing through the branches and brush. To know that the enemies were so close by but not be able to see them nearly drove me insane.

Then, one appeared. It buzzed above us, darting through the trees where it landed on a branch to watch us. Once again, I had that feeling that this wasn't really happening, that I was watching some sort of space age science fiction movie. The monster mosquito couldn't be real, shouldn't be real.

But I knew better. I had a hole in my T-shirt and bug goop all over me to prove it.

Without warning, the mosquito dropped off the branch and came at us. Abby stopped and held up her deck railing, wielding it like a large baseball bat.

I had a better idea.

I stepped in front of her. "I'll get him!" I said. "You be ready, just in case I miss him!"

The mosquito came right at me, unaware of the deadly pitchfork in my hands. Faster and faster he came, in a straight beeline, his stinger extending in front of him like a speeding spear.

I held my ground with the pitchfork raised. The mosquito showed no signs of turning away, and when he had reached me, I made a savage thrust with the pitchfork, stabbing the enormous insect. The bug struggled to free itself, but he couldn't. He stuck to the tines, and I smashed him into the ground where he lay in the weeds, quivering in the throes of death.

"You did it!" Abby said. "You got him!"

"Yeah," I said, feeling a little sense of pride. I pulled the pitchfork from the dead mosquito and wiped the tines in the grass to remove the sticky bug goop. "But that was just one. We have no idea how many there are. If they all try to attack us at once, we'll never have a chance."

Unfortunately for us, that nightmare was about to happen.

20

We had no sooner started out again when the buzzing became even louder, a horrible roaring in our ears. Above us, we began to see movement as the mosquitoes arrived, buzzing over the treetops.

"We've got to get to the house!" I shouted, and my voice was nearly drowned out by the thunder of wings.

We kept going, pushing branches out of our way, hurrying through the underbrush, while the monster mosquitoes circled in the sky like mad vultures. I knew it wouldn't be long before they came after us, and if they all decided to attack at once, we'd never have a chance. There was no way we'd be able to fend off all of them with only a pitchfork and a piece of wood.

One by one, the mosquitoes took turns dipping down toward us. We kept them at bay by swinging our weapons while we moved through the thick foliage. Although it was apparent they really wanted to get us, they were a bit apprehensive. None of the mosquitoes were acting as aggressively as the first three had. Maybe they were aware that we were armed, and that kept them from getting too close.

And we were making progress. We couldn't move very fast, being that we had to keep our eyes peeled and defend ourselves, but we kept moving, and it appeared that we would make it to the house and to safety. I had no idea if anyone was home, or if we could get inside and get away from the mosquitoes, but it was a chance we had to take.

Then, just as we were about to emerge from the woods and into the field, the monster mosquitoes changed their behavior. One of them attacked me with such speed that I just barely had time to block him with the pitchfork. I succeeded only in deflecting him to the side, where his stinger buried deep into a tree. The insect tried desperately to pull out his stinger, and in the process, his wings beat the air like crazy, buzzing like a jet airplane.

"Keep going!" I shouted to Abby.

"I can't go much faster!" Abby said. *"These things keep coming at me!"*

The monster mosquitoes began coming at us two and three at a time. My shoulders and arms were quickly becoming exhausted from swinging the pitchfork. Abby was getting tired, too. It wouldn't be long before our strength was gone, especially if we had to keep fighting as intensely as we were.

Finally, we emerged from the forest, but the

mosquitoes increased their vicious attacks. They buzzed in the air all around us, seeking to plunge their long stingers into our soft flesh. Abby and I were forced to defend ourselves, back to back, swinging our weapons, trying to keep the insects away.

While we fought, we tried to make our way to the house. The problem was that it was nearly impossible to watch where we were going and where we were stepping, because we had to stay so focused on battling the giant mosquitoes.

And as fate would have it, we both accidentally walked into a small tree stump.

I managed to catch myself before I fell down, although I nearly stabbed myself with the pitchfork in the process.

Abby, however, wasn't so fortunate. She fell flat on her face, dropping the piece of railing she had been using to defend herself.

The monster mosquitoes seized the opportunity, but they didn't immediately attack her with their stingers. Two of the insects climbed on top of her. While she struggled to get away and fight them off, the two mosquitoes succeeded in lifting her off the ground!

"*Ray!*" she shrieked. "*Do something! Help me!*"

But the monster mosquitoes were too fast. Besides: I was busy fending them off *me*, and I couldn't take my focus away from the attacking insects. I could do nothing as Abby was carried away by two giant, bloodthirsty mosquitoes.

21

I didn't know what to do. I couldn't throw the pitchfork at the mosquitoes that were carrying Abby away, because I risked hitting her with the sharp tines. On top of that, I needed it for my own defense.

During a moment when the mosquitoes were attacking me, I glanced down and saw a rock that was about the size of my fist.

It was my only chance.

I switched the pitchfork from my right hand to my left, knelt down, grabbed the rock, and stood back up. In one single motion, I drew the rock back, aimed for one of the mosquitoes carrying Abby, and let it fly.

By now, Abby was nearly fifteen feet in the air. If the mosquitoes dropped her, she might break an arm or leg. But it was certainly better than being hauled away by two horrible insects!

Or I might accidentally hit her with the rock, but I didn't think I would. She wasn't that far away. And I'm the pitcher for our baseball team, and I'm pretty good at it.

And all of my pitching experience paid off. The rock hit one of the mosquitoes square in the side of its body, knocking it sideways and tearing away its grip on Abby. The other mosquito was unable to fly with so much weight, but wasn't going to give up. As a result, the insect and Abby began sinking back to earth.

I rushed toward them with my pitchfork and as soon as the insect was within reach, I plunged the sharp tines into its body. The insect let go, and Abby fell only a few feet to the ground, landing on her side. She immediately got up.

"Behind you!" she shrieked, pointing.

I spun with the pitchfork, and just in time. Two mosquitoes were mounting an assault, but I was able to knock them away with the metal tines.

Frantically, I looked around the field, then glanced at the house and the barn while trying to keep the mosquitoes away. By now, Abby had retrieved her piece of the deck railing and was using it to defend herself.

The bad news was that it appeared no one was home. I didn't see any cars in the driveway in front of the house, and all of the window curtains were closed. But there was a smaller shed near the barn, and its door was cracked open a little bit. I was sure we could hide in there and be safe.

"Follow me!" I yelled to Abby.

We ran as best we could while trying to keep the monster mosquitoes from jabbing us with their giant stingers. The sound of their wings continued to roar, but by now, I had gotten used to it.

"Get inside that shed!" I ordered Abby. "I'm right behind you!"

Abby, carrying her piece of wood, shoved the door open and ran inside. I was right behind her, and I wasted no time slamming the metal door behind me. We were immersed in darkness.

Both of us were out of breath, and we didn't speak for a few moments. Finally, I found a wall and leaned my pitchfork against it.

"I wonder if there's a light in here," I said. I tried feeling around the walls, but I didn't find a switch.

"I don't care if there's a light in here or not," Abby said. "At least we're safe."

Outside the shed, the droning sound of beating wings was lessening. It sounded as if the monster mosquitoes were once again leaving.

"Well," Abby began, "it's obvious that *that* plan won't work. No matter where we go, those things are going to come after us. There's just too many of them."

I opened the door a little bit, allowing sunlight to enter the small shed. It was cluttered with all sorts of things: cans, buckets, boxes, garden and yard tools, a rotting garden hose, and a couple of very old bicycles with flat tires.

But it was what was at the back of the shed that drew my attention.

"Abby!" I blurted. *"Look at that! That's just what we need!"*

22

At the back of the shed, buried beneath a pile of junk, was a motorcycle. It didn't appear to be very old, and it wasn't very big, either. In fact, it looked like a motorcycle made for a kid.

I don't own a motorcycle, but my uncle in Michigan has a few of them. We visit him every summer, and he lets me ride around his property on one of the smaller ones. It's a very cool dirt bike, and I'm pretty good at handling it.

"If we can get that thing started," I said excitedly, "that's our ticket out of here. I don't think those mosquitoes would be able to keep up with us. Help me get the stuff off of it."

It didn't take us long to pull away all of the junk from the back of the shed and move it around, allowing enough room to wheel the motorcycle to the middle of the shed.

"Do you think it works?" Abby asked.

I shrugged. "Let's find out," I said, slipping onto the motorcycle seat.

The bike didn't have a key, but it didn't require one. There was an *on/off* switch near the right handlebar grip. I positioned it to the *on* position, then located the kick start on the right side of the motorcycle. I placed my foot on it and pushed down. The engine turned, but it didn't start. I tried it again. Two more times.

Finally, I gave it one strong pump, and the engine roared to life. The throttle was actually the right handlebar grip, and I rolled it back to give the engine some more gas. It responded with a loud whine.

"It works!" I shouted triumphantly. "You can ride behind me, and we can get out of here!"

"Are you sure you know what you're doing?" Abby asked.

"Of course I do," I replied. "My uncle in Michigan let's me drive one of his motorcycles every summer. Hop on. Let's get out of here and get help."

Reluctantly, Abby slipped onto the seat behind me.

"Hold on around my waist," I said. "Things might get a bit bumpy."

"Just for the record," Abby said, "I don't think this is a very good idea."

"We don't have any other options," I pointed out. "Either we try to get out of here, or we stay stuck in the shed until somebody finds us. And that might be a while."

I pulled in the clutch with my fingers. The clutch is similar to a handbrake on a bicycle. It disengages the engine and allows you to shift into different gears.

Using my left foot, I pressed down the gear shift lever and put the motorcycle into first gear. Then, I gently turned the throttle and began to release the clutch. The motorcycle inched forward. When the front wheel was near the door, I pulled in the clutch again and hit the brake. The motorcycle stopped, and I leaned forward and pushed open the door with my right hand. Sunlight flooded in, and I inched the motorcycle out of the shed and into the yard.

We didn't see any monster mosquitoes, but that didn't mean they weren't hiding somewhere nearby, most likely in the trees.

I turned my head and spoke over my shoulder. "Hang on tight," I said. "We're getting out of here."

I cranked back the throttle and released the clutch. The motorcycle surged forward . . . and it was at that very moment that Abby and I were knocked violently off the motorcycle and sent sprawling onto the ground.

23

I found myself on the ground so quickly that I wasn't even aware of what had happened. It didn't occur to me that the monster mosquitoes were responsible for knocking us from the motorcycle and to the ground.

Beside me, Abby had struck the ground on her side and was already getting up. I leapt to my feet to see where the mosquitoes had gone.

There had been two of them. Because of the

sound of the motorcycle engine, we hadn't heard their wings, and we'd had no idea they were around. We were lucky that they hadn't used their stingers. Perhaps that was their plan, but they missed. Either way, we were alive, and I was grateful.

The motorcycle lay on its side. The engine had stalled, and the rear wheel was spinning. I grabbed the handlebars and started to pull it up, but I had to let go when one of the mosquitoes dropped out of the sky, coming right for me. Once again, Abby and I were forced to retreat back into the shed. Even then, one of the mosquitoes tried to get at us, and I had to quickly force the door closed to keep him from getting inside.

"This is getting really, really old," Abby said.

"Tell me about it," I replied. "I never knew we could get into so much trouble by just going to look for a haunted house."

"A haunted house that isn't even haunted," Abby added.

"I guess the best thing for us to do is wait,"

I said. "The problem is, we have no idea how long we'll have to stay here. Sooner or later, when we don't show up at home, our parents will come looking for us."

"But anyone who comes looking for us is going to be attacked by those giant bugs," Abby said.

She had a point. I didn't think very many people, if any, knew about the monster mosquitoes. Anyone searching for us would quickly come under attack.

I opened the shed door a little bit, listening carefully for the sound of buzzing wings. The sunlight was refreshing, and it made me feel less confined. I peered up into the trees to see if I could see any mosquitoes, but there were none. Still, I knew they had to be close, perhaps hiding within the tree branches, blending in with the limbs and leaves, waiting.

"Well," Abby began, "at the very least, we—"

Abby was interrupted by a noise, but it wasn't the sound of flapping wings. This was a totally different sound altogether, the sound of gravel crunching.

I poked my head out of the shed door, and I couldn't believe what I saw.

"It's a car!" I said. *"There's a car coming up the driveway!"*

Finally, it appeared our luck was about to change.

24

The car was a mid-sized, gray four-door and looked a lot like the car my mom drives. It rolled up the driveway and stopped in front of the house, but because of the sun's glare on the windshield, I couldn't see the person driving it.

"I wonder if they know about the mosquitoes," Abby said.

"They will in a minute," I said. "When whoever is driving the car gets out, I'm going to yell to warn them, just in case they don't know."

After a moment, the driver's side door opened, and a woman stepped out. She appeared to be about my mom's age, only with much darker hair.

And she was wearing a white lab coat. I thought that was kind of strange. She looked like she might be a doctor.

"Hey!" I shouted to the woman. "Be careful! There are giant mosquitoes all over the place!"

The woman spun, completely surprised. Her jaw fell, and she looked shocked.

"Who said that?" she asked.

I poked my head out farther and waved.

"Me," I said. "I'm Ray. My friend Abby is with me. We were attacked by giant mosquitoes and had to hide here in your shed."

The woman looked up and around.

"When did you last see them?" she asked.

"Just a few minutes ago," I replied. I pointed at the motorcycle. "Honest, we weren't trying to steal the motorcycle. We were just trying to use it to get away from the mosquitoes. We needed a way to get home, but the mosquitoes knocked us off of it and attacked us again."

"You're both lucky to be alive," the woman said, still eyeing the sky. "I'll unlock the front door to my house. When it's open, make sure there are no mosquitoes around, and then run across the yard and come inside."

The woman hurried, jogging the few feet to her front door and inserting a key in the doorknob. The door opened, and she stepped inside.

"Strange," Abby said.

"What's strange?" I said.

"She didn't sound surprised at all to hear about the giant mosquitoes," Abby said. "If anybody told me they were chased by giant bugs, I would never believe them unless I saw them."

"Maybe she knows something we don't," I said.

"All clear!" the woman shouted from the doorway, waving toward us. "Come inside! Hurry!"

I made one more check, scanning the trees

in the sky to make sure there were no monster mosquitoes ready to assault us. Seeing none, I grabbed Abby's hand.

"Let's go," I said, and I pulled her out of the shed. The two of us sprinted across the yard as fast as we could, nearly diving through the doorway and into the woman's house. Immediately, she closed the door behind us.

The relief I felt at that moment was exhilarating. We were inside the house. We were safe. The mosquitoes couldn't get us.

"What's going on?" Abby asked. "Have you seen those giant mosquitoes?"

The woman looked at Abby, then looked at me.

"Yeah," I said. "Do you know anything about them?"

The woman nodded. "Yes," she said, a bit sheepishly. It was as if she was a little embarrassed.

"What do you know about them?" Abby asked.

"I know *all* about them," the woman replied. "I think I'm the one who created them."

I look at Abby, and she looked at me.

"What do you mean, you *created* them?" I asked.

" Just that," the woman replied. "I created them. Now, I've got to stop them."

"But how do you create giant bugs?" Abby asked.

The woman paused for a moment, sighed, then spoke.

"Perhaps we'd better sit down," she said. "Let's go into the kitchen, and I'll get you each a glass of water. Then, I'll tell you what happened."

We followed her into the kitchen and sat at the table. The woman returned with two glasses of ice water, handing one to each of us. Then, she sat down and began to tell us how she had created this entire mess.

And while she spoke, I began to realize that our nightmare might not be over, after all . . . .

25

The woman's name was Dr. Janet Cornwell, and she was a veterinarian. She told us she had created a special steroid for her horses.

"What's a steroid?" Abby asked.

Dr. Cornwell thought for a moment. "There could be a lot of different answers to that question," she said. "But basically, I use a particular type of steroid to help injured horses, horses that have swelling in their joints or other areas of their bodies."

Abby and I nodded, but I don't think either one of us really understood what she was talking about.

"At my laboratory in the city, I have been working on a special mixture of several different steroids, in hopes of coming up with a super-drug that will be even better than the ones available now."

"But what does this have to do with monster mosquitoes?" I asked.

Dr. Cornwell smiled. "I'm getting to that," she said. "I have a horse that has a sprained ankle," she continued. "I tried a small dose of my new steroid on her. It worked very well, and within twenty-four hours, the swelling in her ankle had gone down a lot.

"But there is a chemical compound within this new steroid that has effects I wasn't aware of. Although the drug is very safe and helpful for horses, it has a very negative effect on other things. Mainly, insects."

"You mean mosquitoes?" I asked.

Dr. Cornwell nodded. "That's exactly what I mean," she said.

"You gave your drug to mosquitoes?" Abby asked. "Why?"

Dr. Cornwell shook her head. "Absolutely not," she said.

Suddenly, I understood exactly what happened.

"The mosquitoes bit your horses!" I said. "When they bit your horses, they sucked up their blood, and the drug went into their bodies, too."

"Exactly," Dr. Cornwell said. "The effect it has on the mosquitoes was something I had no idea about. I never knew something like this would happen."

"Where are your horses now?" Abby asked.

"I had to put them in the barn," Dr. Cornwell replied. "It's the only safe place for them, for the time being. At least until those mosquitoes shrink back to their original size."

"How will that happen?" I asked.

"I think it will only be a matter of time," Dr. Cornwell replied. "I think that once the drug runs its course, it will wear off, and the mosquitoes will gradually become small once again. But until then, we've got a big problem. Because of their enormous size, the mosquitoes are incredibly strong."

"And they have stingers like spears," I said.

Dr. Cornwell nodded. "Exactly," she said. "That makes them particularly dangerous. I have had to be very careful even walking to and from my car."

"But how long will it be before they change back to their original size?" Abby asked.

Dr. Cornwell frowned, and a puzzled look came over her face. "I'm not exactly sure," she replied. "It could be a few hours, it could be a few days. It may take a week or two."

A week or two?!?! I thought. By then, those monster mosquitoes could have seriously hurt someone . . . or worse.

Abby and I explained to Dr. Cornwell how

we had become involved, that we had actually started out our day looking for a haunted house, and that the mosquitoes had attacked us while we were on our way. I told her that we had been trying to get home, but the monster mosquitoes kept coming after us.

"Well," she said, "I think I can help you there. I can give you a ride home in my car. Do you need to use the phone to call your parents?"

I shook my head. "No," I replied. "We aren't late. Besides: I don't want to tell my parents what happened over the phone. They'd think I was making up a story. This is something I want to tell them about in person."

"Same here," Abby said. "If I call up my parents and start telling them about giant mosquitoes attacking me, they'll think I'd gone crazy. They'd want to put me in the looney bin."

"Fine," Dr. Cornwell said. "We'll make sure there aren't any mosquitoes around, and then we can run to my car."

I felt a huge wave of relief. I was glad that

we were safe, that we hadn't been hurt by the monster mosquitoes.

But I was also kind of excited. It had been an incredible adventure, and I couldn't wait to tell my friends and family about it. Plus, I would have a great story to write about when I went back to school in the fall.

We stood. "Thanks for the water," I said.

"Yeah," Abby chimed in. "Thanks."

Unfortunately, we were about to find out that getting home wasn't going to be as easy as we thought, for at the exact moment that we placed the glasses on the counter next to the sink, the kitchen window exploded inward, showering glass everywhere.

26

Although we didn't have any warning, Abby and I were not injured. Several shards of glass hit us, but we were fortunate enough not to get any cuts. The glass fell all around us, clattering to the counter, floor, and the sink.

But I wasn't worried about the glass.

Perched on the windowsill—covering the entire window, in fact—was a giant mosquito. His stinger was so long that the end of it was only inches from our faces.

"Get back!" Dr. Cornwell ordered.

Abby and I raced through the kitchen, around the corner, and into the living room.

Meanwhile, Dr. Cornwell had reached beneath the counter and into a cupboard. She pulled out a black and yellow can of insect killer and held it out at arm's length toward the mosquito.

Just as the insect was about to take flight and attack, Dr. Cornwell sprayed it. A stream of liquid shot out from the can and hit the insect.

The effect was immediate, and the mosquito suddenly stopped fluttering its wings and fell forward, dropping into the kitchen sink with a crash. It quivered and shook for a moment, then stopped. It was dead.

"There's a painting of a mountain on the wall in the living room!" Dr. Cornwell shouted. "Bring it to me! I've got to use it to cover this window before more mosquitoes get in!"

The painting she spoke of was directly in

front of us. Carefully, Abby and I lifted it from the wall and carried it to the kitchen. Dr. Cornwell took it from us and placed it on the shelf beneath the window. The painting was just big enough to cover the entire space.

"That won't hold them for long," she replied. "But it will work for now."

"Can't you just use the insect killer?" Abby asked as she pointed to the can on the counter.

"The spray works great," she said, "but if a lot of mosquitoes attack at the same time, it would be impossible to spray them all. Now . . . let's get to the car and get you two home."

Dr. Cornwell picked up the can of insect killer, and the three of us walked through the living room to the front door. We waited for a moment while she peered out the living room window. I kept waiting for a mosquito to charge the glass and break inside, but thankfully, that never happened.

Then, Dr. Cornwell walked to the front door and opened it a tiny bit. She peered outside.

Satisfied that there were no monster mosquitoes nearby, she opened the door a bit farther, pausing once again to scan the surroundings.

"You never can tell with those things," she said. "They could be just about anywhere."

"Are you sure it's safe to run to your car?" Abby asked.

Dr. Cornwell shook her head. "No," she replied, "it's not safe. I'm going to get the car and then drive up closer to the house. That way, you two won't have to run very far. I'll pull the car up next to the porch. Then, you'll only have a couple of feet to go to get in through the passenger side door."

That sounded easy enough.

It wasn't going to be.

27

Still scanning the area for signs of any mosquitoes, Dr. Cornwell stepped through the doorway and onto the porch, carrying the can of insect killer. Then, she turned to us.

"I'm going to close the door. Don't open the door until the car is next to the porch. I'll push open the passenger door so it will be easy for you to get into the car."

Abby and I nodded. We understood.

Dr. Cornwell closed the door. Through the living room window, we watched her hurry across the porch, into the yard, and over to her car.

"I'll be glad when this is all over," Abby said.

"You and me both," I said. "At least we know where the monster mosquitoes came from and that they're not going to be around forever."

We held our breaths while Dr. Cornwell raced to her car. It was with great relief that we saw her reach the driver's side door and slip inside. Then, she pulled the door shut, and we heard the engine roar to life.

"She made it!" Abby cheered. "I expected one of those crazy bugs to attack her."

"We are as good as home," I said.

Not quite.

Dr. Cornwell's car lurched forward. As it did, a dark form dropped out of the sky. Then another, and another.

Mosquitoes.

One of them landed on the windshield and began to hit the glass with its stinger, tapping like a mad woodpecker. We watched in horror as the long stinger punctured the glass, spider webbing the entire windshield.

The car stopped in the driveway. The other two monster mosquitoes had succeeded in using their stingers to puncture the two front tires. Both were now flat.

"We've got to do something!" Abby said.

"She's got a can of insect killer," I said. "She'll use it. She'll be okay."

I hope, I thought, after I had said those words.

"This nightmare just keeps getting worse and worse," Abby said. "When is it going to be over?"

"Soon," I said.

Back at the car, Dr. Cornwell had rolled down the driver's side window a few inches. She stuck her arm out, and we could see the can of insect killer in her hand. A liquid stream jetted out and hit the mosquito that was on her windshield. Instantly, the giant bug fell over and tumbled to the ground with its long legs in the air. It was dead.

"See?" I said. "Dr. Cornwell knows what she's doing."

"But now the car has two flat tires," Abby said. "We can't use it to get away."

"Dr. Cornwell has a telephone," I reminded her. "We can use it to call for help, if we need to. The first thing we need to do is help Dr. Cornwell. We have to make sure she can get back into the house safely."

"Like you said, she's got the can of bug killer," Abby said. "So, she'll be okay."

While we watched, Dr. Cornwell slowly opened the driver's side door. When she did, both mosquitoes that were still seizing the front tires suddenly flew into the air. Dr. Cornwell was fast and sprayed both of them. They fell to the ground, dead.

Then, she began jogging toward us, back to the house. I stood by the door, ready to open it when she arrived.

Abby screamed, and I looked out the window to see what had happened.

A mosquito had attacked Dr. Cornwell from above and behind. Dr. Cornwell hadn't seen it, and the insect succeeded in snagging her can of bug killer and carrying it away. Another monster mosquito was now nearly upon her, and she was forced to stop and face the attacking insect. But she had nothing to fight it off with except her bare hands.

My eyes darted around the living room, searching for anything I could use as a weapon. There was nothing.

"Maybe there's something in the closet!" Abby said, pointing to a closed door near the couch. I raced toward it and threw open the door.

On the floor were rows and rows of shoes. I've never seen so many shoes in one small room in my life. There was also lots of clothing hanging on hangers.

But in the back, in the corner, was a long broom. It wasn't much, but at least it was something.

I pulled it out.

"A broom?!?!" Abby said. "What are you going to do with *that?*"

"It's the only thing we've got!" I replied. "If we don't do something, those things are going to get her!"

Carrying the broom in my left hand, I threw open the front door and bounded onto the porch.

I was about to run into the yard, to help Dr. Cornwell, when I suddenly realized it wouldn't be necessary.

I was too late.

In the yard, the mosquito had Dr. Cornwell pinned to the ground. She was struggling to get up, but it was no use against the mosquito's incredible strength. In seconds, the insect would plunge his stinger into the doctor . . . and there was nothing anyone could do about it.

28

I did the only thing I could do: using the broom as a spear, I drew it back and hurled the pointed end as hard as I could. I knew there was no time for me to run to her, and I doubted that the broom would do anything to hurt the mosquito, but I had to try.

The broom sailed through the air like a javelin.

The monster mosquito drew his head back and prepared to drive his stinger down.

I missed the insect with the broom, and it landed next to Dr. Cornwell. Although it had little effect on the mosquito, it distracted the giant bug long enough for Dr. Cornwell to pick up the broom. She began hitting the insect with the handle, thrashing madly back and forth. The insect released his grip and flew into the air, hovering a few feet above her.

This gave Dr. Cornwell enough time to get to her feet. Still holding the broom, she wielded it before her, swinging at the enormous mosquito buzzing above her head.

But she wasn't safe yet. More giant insects appeared in the sky, emerging over the treetops and descending into the yard.

"Dr. Cornwell!" I shouted. "They're coming for you! Get inside, quick!"

Dr. Cornwell began backing up toward the house. She couldn't turn and run because the mosquito was still after her, and she needed to use the broom to keep it away. When she reached the porch, she nearly tripped, but I grabbed her arm and helped steady her. The two of us leapt through the doorway and into the living room. Abby, who had been watching the horrifying scene, was ready. She slammed the front door and locked it.

"Those things are much stronger than I thought," Dr. Cornwell said. She was out of breath and gasping heavily. "They're also a lot smarter than I imagined. They knew how to stop the car by puncturing the tires."

Super-intelligent insects? I thought. I had always imagined mosquitoes to be pretty dumb. I mean, when one landed on you, it was easy enough to smack it and kill it.

But these mosquitoes? Not only were they super strong, they were smart . . . and that scared me. Somehow, I knew that these menacing monster mosquitoes were going to use their intelligence against us.

And I was right.

29

Dr. Cornwell hurried into the kitchen.

"Keep away from the doors and windows," she said. "I'm not sure what those things are capable of doing."

To my great relief, I watched her pick up the telephone. She was going to call for help. I was sure the police would arrive soon. I didn't know what they would do, but they would have guns and rifles. They would be able to shoot the mosquitoes out of the sky.

Dr. Cornwell frowned and pulled the phone away from her ear. She held it out, looking at it with a puzzled look on her face.

"What's wrong?" Abby asked.

Dr. Cornwell looked dumbfounded. "The phone," she said, bewildered. "It's dead. The mosquitoes must've drilled through the phone lines."

"Don't you have a cell phone?" I asked.

"Yes," she replied. "But it's in the car."

Outside, we could hear the buzzing of insects growing louder. There were scratching sounds, like they were landing on the roof.

"What if they get into the house?" Abby asked. "They can break the windows and get inside."

"Let's get down into the basement," Dr. Cornwell said. "But first, let's find something to defend ourselves, just in case."

"Do you have any guns?" I asked.

Dr. Cornwell shook her head. "My husband

has a shotgun," she replied, "but it's locked in a cabinet, and I don't know where he keeps the key."

"Won't he be home soon?" Abby asked.

Again, the doctor shook her head. "He's on a business trip to New York," she replied. "He won't be home for a couple of days."

Dr. Cornwell began rummaging through the kitchen. From another closet, she pulled out a mop and handed it to me.

"Here," she said.

If the situation hadn't been so serious, I would've laughed out loud. Who would believe we were being attacked by giant mosquitoes and I had just been given a mop to fight them with?

Crazy.

In the same closet, the doctor found another broom.

"I think this is about all I've got," she said. "Now, let's get to the basement."

The basement door was at the far end of the house, at the other end of a long hallway.

I had noticed that the buzzing sound all

around the house was getting louder and louder. It sounded like there were mosquitoes all around us, and I was thankful that we were indoors. If we were outside, I think we wouldn't have stood a chance.

Suddenly, explosions of glass shattered in every room of the house.

"They're all attacking at once!" Dr. Cornwell shouted. "They've smashed all of the windows! We've got to hurry!"

The three of us sprinted down the hall with Dr. Cornwell carrying the broom and me carrying the mop. Abby didn't have anything; she was defenseless.

Suddenly, a mosquito appeared in the hall ahead of us. No doubt it'd broken through one of the bedroom windows to gain access to the house.

Behind us, two monster mosquitoes were hovering in the hallway. We couldn't reach the basement, and now, we couldn't go back.

There was only one thing we could do.

We had to fight.

30

There's a game we play at school called *Monkey in the Middle*.

That's kind of what I felt like at that moment, except this time, there were three monkeys in the middle . . . and the game had turned deadly.

"I'll take on these two behind us," Dr. Cornwell said. "Ray, you handle the one in front of us. Abby, you don't have a weapon, so you stay in the middle, between the two of us."

Dr. Cornwell and I sandwiched Abby between us with our backs to her. I held up the mop; the doctor wielded the broom.

The three of the monster mosquitoes came at us, and fast. I was lucky enough to knock the one that attacked me to the floor, where I begin hitting it with the mop, over and over and over. When the insect finally stopped moving, I turned around to help Dr. Cornwell. Once, the mosquito struck out with its stinger and nearly drove it into her shoulder, but she ducked aside just in time. I knocked it to the floor, and she finished him off.

But we knew it wasn't over. We could hear other mosquitoes in the house. They had broken through the windows and were searching for us.

"Now!" Dr. Cornwell ordered. *"Follow me to the basement."*

We sprinted the rest of the way down the hall, rounded the corner, and found the basement door. Dr. Cornwell flung it open and flicked on the light. She stood aside and urged us to go down the stairs.

"Be careful on the steps," she said as we quickly brushed past her. Then, she closed the door behind her and followed us down the stairs.

"We'll be safe down here," the doctor said. "There are no windows for them to break through."

Abby spoke. "If you would've told me this morning that I'd be hiding in the basement to keep away from mosquitoes, I would've said that you are crazy."

"You're not crazy," the doctor said. "None of us are. I would've never imagined something like this happening."

"Now what?" I asked.

"We wait," Dr. Cornwell replied. "We wait for the drug to wear off. The mosquitoes will return to their normal size after a while."

"How long is a while?" Abby asked. "If I'm not home for dinner, my parents are going to get worried. They're going to come looking for me, and I don't want them to get attacked by those flying freaks."

"I wish I had an answer for you," Dr. Cornwell replied, shaking her head. "But I just don't know."

Even in the basement, we could hear the buzzing of the mosquitoes. The droning sound was all around us, and it felt like it was shaking the walls and the foundations of the house. We had been very lucky to make it to the basement when we did, as it was the only safe place in the house.

But that also meant something else: there was no way we could get out except through the basement door, and we couldn't get out that way because of the mosquitos in the house. So, for the time being, there was no way out, which was fine. At least we were safe.

However, when the basement door began to shudder and shake, when the monster mosquitoes began their furious, all-out assault to break down the door, I knew that our safe place in the basement was about to become our tomb.

31

When we heard the loud noise at the top of the stairs on the other side of the door, the buzzing and scratching, we weren't worried . . . at first.

But when the door started shaking, and we could hear wood splintering, that's when we started to panic. Even Dr. Cornwell was completely shocked.

"No!" she exclaimed. "It's not possible! They can't be that strong!"

"Can they break down the door?!?!" Abby shrieked.

"I'm not sure," the doctor replied. "But we've got to make sure they don't. If they get into the basement, we have nowhere to go."

Dr. Cornwell bolted up the stairs, and Abby and I followed. The sound coming from the other side of the door was horrifying: not only could we hear the buzzing of mosquito wings, but they were doing everything they could to break down the door. It sounded like they were hitting it with their stingers and shaking it with their legs. I didn't know how many mosquitoes there were, but I was sure I didn't want to find out.

Dr. Cornwell placed her hands against the door and used her weight to push on it. Abby and I did the same. We could feel the door trembling and shaking, and once again, I thought about how crazy it was that we were trying to fend off gigantic insects.

The wood continued splintering as the hinges began to give way.

"They're going to break the door down!" I shouted.

"Keep pressing against it!" Dr. Cornwell ordered. "We can't let them in! We can't let them break in!"

The door continued to shudder and shake violently. The pounding continued, as did the loud buzzing. There was more splintering of wood as the door began to come away from the molding.

"It's no use!" Abby said. "They're going to get in!"

We felt a sudden surge as the door was finally torn from its hinges. All three of us were knocked off balance, but somehow, none of us fell down the steps. The door tumbled down a couple of stairs, then fell to the side.

The three of us ran down the stairs. Dr. Cornwell picked up the broom, and I picked up the mop. We raced to an empty corner of the basement and prepared to defend ourselves.

The monster mosquitoes poured down the stairs. Several of them were flying, but a few more were crawling. All of them displayed their long, needle-like stingers, their long javelins of death.

There's no way we can fend off this many, I thought. *We might be able to fight a couple of them, but there is no way we can stop this many giant mosquitoes.*

I was filled with horror and sadness. My short life was going to come to an end in the basement of someone else's house, and there was nothing I could do about it.

32

The three of us were backed into the corner as far as we could go, pressing up against one another. I could feel Abby shaking next to me on my left. On my right, Dr. Cornwell's body was stiff and rigid as she prepared to defend us with the broom. I held out the mop to try to knock away any mosquitoes, but I knew it was no use. There was just too many.

But then, a strange thing began to happen.

At first, the mosquitoes lined up, as if they

were all going to charge us at the same time. There were even a few mosquitoes on the ground, crawling toward us. I counted eleven of them.

Suddenly, one of the flying mosquitoes fell to the ground on his own. He landed on his legs, but he had a difficult time standing. The insect began wobbling back and forth, unstable, and I thought he was going to fall down. Soon, other mosquitoes were doing the same thing. Even the ones that hadn't been flying, the ones that had been crawling, were acting funny.

While we watched, the mosquitoes began to shrink! They began to get smaller and smaller. The process was slow, but within a couple of minutes, the insects were half their size. Some of them were still able to fly, but they, too, had shrunk.

"The drug is finally wearing off!" Dr. Cornwell said. "It's finally wearing off, and they're returning to their normal size!"

Still, we remained in the corner, ready to defend ourselves if necessary. However, the mosquitoes continued to shrink, and after about fifteen minutes, they were a mere fraction of their gargantuan size. In fact, most of them were now smaller than a dime, and they buzzed about harmlessly in the basement.

"Did that just happen?" Abby asked in amazement. "Did I just see those monster mosquitoes shrink right before my very eyes?"

"Yes, you did," Dr. Cornwell replied. "And just in the nick of time, too. We would have never been able to fight off all of those mosquitoes at the same time."

"This has been the craziest day of my entire life," I said, shaking my head.

"Mine, too," Abby said as a small mosquito lit on her arm. She slapped it. "That's the way you kill mosquitoes," she said. "I don't ever want to have to deal with mosquitoes bigger than that."

"I'm so glad no one was hurt," Dr. Cornwell said. "I would offer to give you both a ride home, but I'm going to need to get my front tires fixed before I drive anywhere."

"That's okay," I said. "Our bicycles are

waiting for us in the woods near the swamp. We'll go get them, now that we don't have to worry about giant mosquitoes attacking us."

Later, when we finally returned to my house, I said good-bye to Abby. Then, I put my bike in the garage and ran into the house to tell Mom and Dad about the giant mosquitoes. I showed them my bug goop-stained shirt and the hole created by the mosquito's stinger. At first, my parents didn't believe me . . . but later that evening, there was a news story on television. Dr. Cornwell was being interviewed, and she was talking about the monster mosquitoes. As it turns out, other people saw them, too, and there were even some pictures shown.

Mom and Dad couldn't believe it.

"I told you," I said. "It was a nightmare."

"You and Abby are very lucky," Mom said. "I hope that veterinarian doesn't try any more experimental drugs for her horses."

The next day, I rode my bike over to Abby's house. We talked a lot about what had happened to us the day before and how lucky we had been. Abby told me she had already started writing a book about the adventure.

"Let's ride our bikes to the convenience store and get a candy bar," I said.

Abby was agreeable to that, so we took off. It was sunny and bright once again, and it was going to be a perfect day to spend outside.

Until a sudden shadow darkened the street. Something big was directly above us, and it was then that we realized that our ordeal with monster mosquitoes wasn't over.

33

Both Abby and I looked up at the same time, expecting to see a monster mosquito coming down at us with its stinger of death, and we turned our bikes sharply to get out of its way.

Imagine our relief when all we saw was an ordinary crow! The shadow it created made us both think the worst.

"I thought that was one of those giant mosquitoes!" Abby said with a laugh. "It really freaked me out."

"Me, too," I said. "I'm sure glad it wasn't."

We bicycled to the convenience store, parked our bikes by a tree, and went inside. We bought two candy bars and two bottles of water, then returned to our bikes. While we sat on our seats sipping water and eating, a girl approached us. She was about our age, with short, dark hair.

"Excuse me," she said. "I'm sorry to bother you, but have you seen a kid around here about this tall?" She raised her hand up, palm down, to about the top of her shoulder. "He's my brother, and sometimes he thinks it's funny to hide from me."

I shook my head. "I haven't seen him," I said.

"Me, neither," Abby replied. "But we'll help you look for him, if you want."

"Sure," the girl said. "But you have to be on the lookout. He likes to jump out and scare people when they least expect it."

"I don't think anything is going to scare me

today," I said, glancing at Abby. "Not after what happened yesterday."

"Yeah," Abby said. "In fact, I think I've had my share of getting scared for a long time."

"What happened yesterday?" the girl asked.

We told her about the giant mosquitoes and the ordeal we'd been through. She listened, amazed.

"That sounds scary," she said, "but it's nothing compared to what I went through."

I looked at Abby, and she looked at me.

"What happened to you?" I asked the girl.

"Yeah," Abby chimed in. "What could be scarier than bloodthirsty, man-eating monster mosquitoes?"

"I'll tell you what," the girl said. "My friends and I were nearly killed by dinosaurs in South Dakota."

I gasped. "I saw that on the news!" I exclaimed. "I heard and read all about it. You were there?!?!"

The girl nodded. "I wish I wasn't, but I was.

It was the most terrifying thing that's ever happened to me."

She began to tell us what happened, and we forgot all about looking for her brother. Instead, Abby and I stood in silence, listening to the girl tell us all about the savage dinosaurs of South Dakota.

Next:

AMERICAN CHILLERS

America's #1 Series for MAXIMUM Chills!

#34: Savage Dinosaurs of South Dakota

Continue on for a FREE preview!

"Hey, Autumn!"

I turned when I heard my name, already recognizing the voice and knowing who it was: Brady Vanguard, a friend I'd met only a few months before. He and his family moved into the house across the street from ours, and he was in fifth grade, the same grade as me. Like me, he also has dark hair, and we are about the same height.

We like a lot of the same things, too,

especially when it comes to food. My favorite food in the whole world is pizza, and so is his. He also loves ice cream, and so do I. We both like school, but we don't like homework. And we both love the movies.

And something we're both fascinated with is dinosaurs. As a matter of fact, that's how we got to know each other. In class one day, he saw a dinosaur book on my desk.

"That looks like a cool book," he said.

"Do you want to take a look at it?" I asked.

His eyes lit up. "I'd love to," he said.

I handed the book to Brady, and he flipped through it.

"These drawings and paintings are really awesome," he said.

"There's a ton of information in there, too" I said. "You can borrow it, if you want. My parents got it for me as a birthday gift. I've already read it once, but I carry it around with me because I like to look at the pictures."

Brady looked at me. "Really? You'd let me

borrow it?" he asked.

"Sure," I replied. "I mean, you just moved into the house across the street. If you don't give it back, I know where to find you." I smiled, and Brady smiled back.

"Thanks," he said. "I promise to return it."

Ever since, we've been good friends. We worked together on a school project in which we had to make dioramas. Our diorama featured dinosaurs; specifically, dinosaurs from the Mesozoic era. We worked on that project a lot: before school, during school, and even after school. Sometimes, we worked together on the weekends.

But are efforts paid off, and we both received an 'A' for our diorama.

Now, he was running up the street, shouting my name. When I turned, I saw him stop at the curb, look both ways, and began to sprint across. He was carrying a newspaper.

"You're not going to believe this!" he said excitedly. "I don't even believe it myself!"

"What?" I asked.

By the time he reached me, he was out of breath. He'd probably been running a couple of blocks.

"This!" he said. "Check this out!" He handed me the newspaper.

I glanced at the headlines and looked at the picture. Then I read the caption next to it.

My mouth fell open, and I think my heart skipped a beat.

"No way!" I said. "Is this for real?"

Brady bobbed his head. "As far as I can tell," he said. "It's not April first, so it's not an April fools joke. I think it's really going to happen."

I studied the article intently, and I couldn't believe what I was reading.

The newspaper article was about an eccentric inventor and entrepreneur who planned to build a Dinosaur Park in Rapid City, South Dakota, which is where we live. That's right: a Dinosaur Park. A couple of years ago, I saw a movie on television that was very similar. In the movie, the dinosaurs were actual clones of dinosaurs, so they were alive and real.

But this inventor wasn't going to build a

park with *live* dinosaurs. All of the dinosaurs in his park were going to be mechanical, although he said they would look and move like real creatures. The difference being, of course, that the dinosaurs wouldn't need to eat food. They would all be powered by rechargeable batteries and programmed by computers.

"This sounds like something right out of the book," I said as I finished reading the article.

"Or a movie," Brady said. "Do you remember that movie about the live dinosaurs in the park?"

"I was just thinking of that while I read the article," I replied, and I pointed at the newspaper. "This park sounds a lot safer, being that the dinosaurs won't be alive."

"They sure look real," Brady said as he scanned the picture on the front page. It was a black-and-white photograph of two dinosaurs: a spinosaurus and a prosauropod. Although the pictures weren't in color, the dinosaurs appeared to be very real-looking.

My imagination went into overdrive. *A*

dinosaur park! I thought. *Right here, in Rapid City! How cool is that going to be?*

The inventor's name was Samuel Putnam, and he said he wanted to build the park for two reasons. First, to satisfy his love and fascination with dinosaurs. Second, he hoped to bring tourists to the area to enjoy the park and learn about the prehistoric lifestyles of the creatures. People could even get their pictures taken next to some of the most ferocious dinosaurs to ever walk the face of the earth! He said that since the dinosaurs were controlled by computers and weren't alive, it would be a very safe family attraction.

And I believed him. Brady believed him. I think everyone who read the article probably believed him. Even Mr. Putnam himself believed that. I'm certain that, in his heart and in his mind, he really thought his dinosaur park would be safe for everyone.

He was dead wrong.

3

Construction on the dinosaur park began later that month. The location was an empty field not far from the city. The project wasn't expected to be complete for nearly a year, and that drove Brady and I crazy. We were *so* anxious for the park to open. I even wrote a letter to Mr. Putnam himself, asking if Brady and I could purchase the first tickets and be the first customers to visit the park. I went to the mailbox every day waiting for a return letter, but I never got one.

No matter. I figured Mr. Putnam was a very busy man, and he had to spend all of his time working on his park and his mechanical, computerized dinosaurs.

One day, there was an article in the newspaper about the project, giving an update on how it was coming along. Surprisingly, they were ahead of schedule, and Mr. Putnam said that they might open two months early, on April 24th instead of June 24th. I marked it on my calendar, and every day that went by I placed an X on that particular date.

Brady and I became even more fascinated with dinosaurs. I think the dinosaur park helped fuel our imaginations. We wondered what kinds of dinosaurs Mr. Putnam had created for his park, and if they would really look and move like actual dinosaurs.

"I think they'll look like the real thing," Brady said one day. "My dad says that scientists and inventors and engineers can do amazing things with robotics these days. That's pretty much what those dinosaurs are going to be: robots."

"I wonder if people will have to control them with a remote, or if they'll be programmed by a computer?" I said.

"They'll probably be programmed, each with its own individual computer," Brady speculated. "That way, he wouldn't have to hire very many workers. Just a couple of computer programmers would be all he would need."

"He might even do the computer programming himself," I said. "He sure sounds like a smart man."

"He's more than just smart," Brady said. "The guy's a genius. If he can figure out a way to make dinosaurs look and act like the real thing, like they really *are* alive, he's probably one of the smartest men on the planet."

The days passed slowly, and every day I put an X on my calendar. It drove me crazy. It was only March, and April 24th seemed a lifetime away.

But on the last day of March, something happened that was going to have a profound effect on my life.

It was Tuesday. I had walked to school, just like every other weekday. Brady and I walked home together, grumbling about the homework we'd been assigned. Not only homework, but math homework. The absolute worst kind of homework.

When we got to our houses, I said goodbye to Brady and walked to the mailbox. I flopped open the metal door and looked inside. There was only one letter there, which seemed a little odd. Usually, the mailbox is filled with letters. Sure, it's mostly junk mail, but it's a rare day when there's only one letter in the mailbox.

I reached in and pulled it out.

It was addressed to me, which was strange. I hardly ever get any mail except around my birthday.

And this was hand-written, too. Someone had sent me a hand-written letter.

Strange.

But even stranger—and much more exciting—was the name on the return address.

Mr. Samuel Putnam.

I tore open the envelope, and what I read made me more excited than anything else I'd ever experienced in my life.

Breathless, I read the letter.

Dear Ms. McLachlan,

I apologize for taking so long to reply to your letter, but I have been very busy working on my dinosaur park project, and have had no time to respond to anyone.

I am thrilled that you are just as excited as I am about my new endeavor. I'm not sure if you saw the article in the newspaper or not, but construction of the park is ahead of schedule, and we will be opening in a few weeks, on April 24th. I will be hosting a grand opening with free food and beverages, tours, as well as souvenir prizes.

In your letter, you asked if you and your friend, Brady, could be the first to attend. It will be my pleasure to welcome both of you to my new park, and I will reserve the first two tickets in your names. When you get to the box office at the entrance of the park, simply tell them who you are, and they will take care of the rest.

I hope you enjoy my dinosaur park. I have been working toward this project since I was a little boy, and it is very rewarding and fulfilling to see my dream come true.

Very truly yours,

Samuel Putnam

I held the letter in my hands and realized

that I was shaking. Then, I read it all over again.

I couldn't believe it! I had forgotten all about the letter I'd sent to Mr. Putnam, figuring he was to busy to get back to me. But he finally had sent me a letter! Not only that, but he agreed to my request! Brady and I were going to be the first two kids to visit the dinosaur park!

Instead of going home, I ran to Brady's house. I pounded on the door so hard that they must've thought someone was trying to break in.

Mrs. Vanguard opened the door in surprise.

"Why, Autumn," she said. "What's the matter?"

"Mrs. Vanguard!" I said, "is Brady home?" Which was a silly question. I'd watched him go into the house only moments before.

By then, Brady had already reached the front door. His mother silently backed away, and Brady stepped forward.

"What's up, Autumn?" he asked.

I waived the letter in front of his face. "This!" I said excitedly. "This is what's up!"

"What is it?" he asked as I handed him the letter.

"Read it!" I said.

Brady held the letter in front of his face, and I watched his lips move in silence as he read the letter. Slowly, his eyes began to widen. I could see the excitement growing on his face.

When he was finished he lowered the letter.

"We are going to be the first people to visit the dinosaur park!" he shouted.

We started jumping up and down. Mrs. Vanguard reappeared in the living room, an expression of surprise on her face.

"What's all the ruckus about?" she asked.

"We're going to the dinosaur park, Mrs. Vanguard!" I said.

"Yeah, Mom!" Brady chimed. "Not only are we going to the dinosaur park, but Mr. Putnam says we can be the first two kids to visit!"

"Who is Mr. Putnam?" Mrs. Vanguard asked.

"He's the inventor who's building the park," I replied. "The dinosaur park has been a dream of his since he was little. I wrote him a letter, asking if Brady and I could be the first two kids to visit the park when it opens. I didn't get anything back from him, so I thought he forgot about my letter. Well, he didn't. I got this letter in the mail today."

Brady was still holding the letter, and he handed it to his mother. Mrs. Vanguard took it from him and she read it. When she finished, she smiled and handed it back to me.

"It sounds like you two are in for an exciting day," Mrs. Vanguard said.

And she was right. Our visit to the dinosaur park would be filled with excitement.

But sometimes, excitement doesn't mean having fun. Sometimes excitement can mean the opposite.

And sometimes, excitement can be disastrous . . . as we were about to find out.

ABOUT THE AUTHOR

Johnathan Rand has been called 'one of the most prolific authors of the century.' He has authored more than 75 books since the year 2000, with well over 4 million copies in print. His series include the incredibly popular **AMERICAN CHILLERS, MICHIGAN CHILLERS, FREDDIE FERNORTNER, FEARLESS FIRST GRADER**, and **THE ADVENTURE CLUB.** He's also co-authored a novel for teens (with Christopher Knight) entitled **PANDEMIA**. When not traveling, Rand lives in northern Michigan with his wife and three dogs. He is also the only author in the world to have a store that sells only his works: **CHILLERMANIA!** is located in Indian River, Michigan and is open year round. Johnathan Rand is not always at the store, but he has been known to drop by frequently. Find out more at:

www.americanchillers.com

Johnathan Rand travels internationally for school visits and book signings! For booking information, call:

1 (231) 238-0338!

www.americanchillers.com

Dont Miss:

WRITTEN AND READ ALOUD BY JOHNATHAN RAND! AVAILABLE ONLY ON COMPACT DISC!

Beware! This special audio CD contains six bone-chilling stories written and read aloud by the master of spooky suspense! American Chillers author Johnathan Rand shares six original tales of terror, including *The People of the Trees, The Mystery of Coyote Lake, Midnight Train, The Phone Call, The House at the End of Gallows Lane,* and the chilling poem, *Dark Night.* Turn out the lights, find a comfortable place, and get ready to enter the strange and bizarre world of **CREEPY CAMPFIRE CHILLERS!**

ONLY 9.99!
over sixty minutes
of audio!

Order online at
www.americanchillers.com
or call toll-free: 1-888-420-4244!

JOIN THE FREE AMERICAN CHILLERS FAN CLUB!

It's easy to join . . . and best of all, it's FREE!
Find out more today by visiting:

WWW.AMERICANCHILLERS.COM

And don't forget to browse the on-line superstore, where you can order books, hats, shirts, and lots more cool stuff!

All AudioCraft books are proudly printed, bound, and manufactured in the United States of America, utilizing American resources, labor, and materials.

USA